DEATH AT THE LAST CHAPTER

MICHAEL N. WILTON

Published 2021 by Next Chapter

Edited by Sheryl Lee

Cover art by CoverMint

CONTENTS

1

A PERSONAL ASSIGNMENT

'Here we are.' Robert Bruce applied the brakes and killed the engine with a sigh of relief, bringing the van to a halt. 'Rose Lodge.' He peered up at the imposing frontage, almost hidden from view by a mass of roses curling up around the front door.

'You sure this is the last one?' asked his friend Gus sleepily, stirring himself and hiding a yawn. 'I've been up since six.'

'Relax, almost finished.' Robert thumbed through his list, ticking it off. 'There we are, my friend's place. Tom Conway, Rose Lodge. You should know it by now, we've been here enough times. Out you get.' He clambered out and stretched. 'Last one.'

Opening the back, he ducked his head inside and pulled out a box, checking over the delivery list. 'Now then,' he said, scanning through the items, 'everything here, except – wait a minute, what happened to the tomato ketchup?'

'Don't ask me, I expect they've run out.'

'But it's his favourite. He always asks for that.'

'Well, don't expect me to go back for it,' his friend grumbled. 'He'll just have to wait until next week – they don't pay us overtime at Home Stores, you should know that by now. You don't need the money – I do.'

'Let's hope he doesn't notice,' replied Robert, ignoring his last remark as he heaved out the box and handed it over, before closing the door. 'I know, I'll ask him how his latest book's getting on. That might do the trick.'

'As long as that old battle-axe of a sister of his doesn't show her face. I can't stand the sight of her.'

'Cheer up, she's probably out having her hair done, if I know her. Come on, let's get it over.'

Gus grinned knowingly. 'Don't kid me – it's that bird of his you're keen on.'

Robert flushed and took hold of the bag to change the subject. 'Here, let me – mind what you're doing with that. Nothing of the sort. Jill's not his bird, you ass; she's his secretary.'

His friend winked. 'Oh yes, I've seen you giving her the eye when he's not looking.'

'That's enough of that. Don't forget it's the side door,' reminded Robert as he led the way.

'Mind the blasted roses,' grumbled his friend. 'Tore my hands in shreds last time I was here.'

'Wouldn't like to be his gardener,' agreed Robert. 'Must be a nightmare looking after that lot. Here, you hold this while I ring.'

They were interrupted by a bicycle pulling up alongside and the cheery voice of the postman announcing his arrival. 'S'cuse me, gents. Why bless me, if it ain't Master Robert.' He doffed his hat respectfully. 'Here, I must tell you ... our Maisie's over the top because of them piano lessons you paid for. Been pestering the life out of me, she has. As if I could afford such goings on, I told her, on my salary – even if it is your birthday, young madam.'

He turned to Gus, seeing his look of surprise. 'Proper knight in shining armour your chum is. Paid for her next term's lessons without batting an eyelid, I ask you. Whole street's buzzing about him and his good deeds. Robert the Bruce, they call him, after that there Scottish King, they do say.'

Robert interrupted hastily. 'Hadn't you better be going, Jim? I think that's someone coming.'

But their gossipy friend was not to be put off that easily and he turned to Gus, eager to spread the word. 'He didn't tell you about last week at the labour exchange either, I bet. Slipping those poor devils a tenner each to keep them going, that's him all right.'

Luckily, and to Robert's relief, they heard the approach of footsteps and Jim hurriedly handed over the post. 'Can't afford to stop here gossiping, gents. Give Mr Conway my regards, will you? I'm off.'

'Well, I'll be ...' Gus was overcome at the thought of doing all that overtime while his friend was happily giving away half his wages.

'And I thought we were mates. Robert the Bruce, eh?' he teased, with a hint of reproach. 'You never told me.'

Before Robert could think up an answer, the door opened and Tom Conway himself stood there, beaming at them.

'Ah, there you are, lads. Come on in. Don't worry about your shoes,' he added as they hesitated. He waved a hand. 'Put it on the table. It's Cook's afternoon off so I'll take care of it. That's the ticket,' he said as Gus dumped the box down thankfully. 'You look as if you could do with a drink. Help yourself.'

Gus licked his lips. 'Wouldn't say no to one of those, sir.' He eyed the nearest bottle of beer eagerly.

'Robert?'

Before he could answer, someone tapped on the door behind them and the gardener stood there, twisting his cap. 'Beg pardon, sir.'

'Don't stand on ceremony, Bates. Plenty there, get yourself a glass.'

'T'wer'n't that, sir. I was wondering if I might beg a favour, like.'

'Well, cough it up. No need for introductions. You've met our delivery friends before now. What's up? Foxes getting at the hens again?'

'No, nothing like that, sir. It's my cousin Nora, sir. Nurse says she's been calling for me – really bad with the flu, she is. Just wondered if I could take some time off and go and see what's up?'

'Of course, man. You don't have to ask. Let me know if there's anything I can do. Let me see, she's at Longbridge if I remember rightly, about ten miles away. Need any transport?'

'No, thank 'e sir. I've got my old truck round the back.'

'Then off you go. Don't hurry back and let me know how she is.'

As the door closed behind him, their host explained gruffly, 'Best gardener we've ever had, that man. Wouldn't refuse him anything.' Seeing them waiting uncertainly, he urged, 'Don't stand on ceremony, drink up.' He eyed Gus's empty glass. 'Oh, I see you have. Have another, there's plenty more; you deserve it after all that delivery business. Too hot for doing anything, this weather.'

Gus shuffled his feet, casting a longing glance at the row of bottles. 'Much as I'd like to, sir, I'd best be off, if you don't mind.' Turning to Robert, he explained apologetically. 'Just remembered, I promised my Lilly I'd take her to the flicks tonight and, if I don't go now, I'll never make it. D'you mind if I take the van? Otherwise I'll be cutting it a bit fine.'

Robert pushed him on his way with a laugh. 'Go on then.' He added jokingly, 'I thought you told me it was Jenny last week?'

'That was last week. This one's a real corker.'

'That's what you said last time.'

'This one's the *real* thing. You sure? I mean about the van.'

'Yes, I've promised to drop something off to someone in the High Street. The walk will do me good.'

'Oh yes?' His friend couldn't resist a parting dig. 'Another of your good deeds – called Jill, isn't she?' He hurriedly escaped, shutting the door behind him before his friend could retaliate.

'Sorry about that,' Robert apologised.

'Don't take any notice; he's only pulling your leg. Come in the den and tell me all your news.'

When they were comfortably settled, he held out a bottle. 'What about a top-up?'

Robert started to relax. 'Just as well I'm not driving. Yes, please.'

'Now, what have you been getting up to,' his host began as he poured a liberal helping. 'Still haven't decided about the job that solicitor of yours was on about? Good steady income I would have thought – what's the problem?'

Robert grimaced. 'I know it sounds awfully ungrateful, but,' he hesitated and sighed, 'spending all day working in a solicitor's office is not my idea of fun.' He tried to explain himself. 'I did try, honest. After Dad died, his partner Henry Arbuthnot went out of his way to encourage me and invited me to join the practice, and his offer still stands I know, but the trouble was ... I found it deadly boring.'

His host laughed in sympathy. 'I know what you mean. I get the same feeling whenever I go and see him.' He poked at the fire thoughtfully. 'What would you like to do if you had the choice?'

Robert took another sip as he considered the idea. 'I suppose anything that doesn't involve routine office work, something I could get my teeth into. Although there's not much chance of anything like that going on around here.'

'Meanwhile, you're quite content to hand out half your

wages, acting as the good Samaritan.' He shook his head. 'That's all very well, but if you ask me, it's time you settled down and found yourself a good woman. Now that's a coincidence,' he observed, struck by a sudden thought. 'My secretary's called Jill – not the same one your friend mentioned?'

Robert spilt some of his drink at the sound of her name and spluttered. 'Sorry about that, my fault.' Dabbing at the spot, he replied hurriedly, managing to keep his voice steady, 'No such luck. She's already promised, I'm told.'

'Don't worry,' said Tom reassuringly, 'plenty more where that came from. Yes, to someone called Ronald Chambers, so she tells me. A local chap, standing for the next by-election, I believe.' Aware that he may have touched on a sensitive subject, he asked casually, 'So, how does that leave you?'

'I'm okay,' said Robert hastily, setting his glass down. 'I have enough to live on, what with the money Dad left me, if that's what you meant. Meanwhile, if I can help some other poor devil down on his luck, I'll do what I can. But I can't see myself getting married on what I get, even if anyone would have me,' he finished with a laugh.

Giving the fire another poke to cover the awkward pause, Tom Conway changed the subject. 'Have you ever thought of following in your uncle's footsteps? In the police, I mean. I know he's retired now, but he was a detective sergeant before that and a damn fine one, as we all know. He should be able to put in a good word for you if you ask him.'

'No thanks. The idea of having to work under someone like that inspector of his gives me the creeps.' He shuddered.

Tom got up and topped up the drinks. 'I dare say. Now, I know they never got on together, largely because that idiot Platt went out of his way to block your uncle's promotion, quite unjustly, I might add, as well you know, but this situation you've got yourself into is a complete waste of your talents.'

He eyed his young friend's well-knit figure with approval.

'Look here, I've always considered myself a good judge of character. I still remember what a splendid job you did, finding out about that previous secretary of mine, who nearly swindled me out of a fortune while he was with me, before I was lucky to land up with young Ji...' He corrected himself hastily, to spare his friend's embarrassment. 'I mean my present one.'

'That was just good luck I came across those faked accounts of his when I did,' allowed Robert modestly.

'Don't kid me. It was sheer hard work, coupled with a touch of genius. Look here,' his host began, coming to a decision, 'I believe I might have just the job for you, if you're interested.'

'What kind of work would that be?' asked Robert cautiously, fearing prospects of another desk job.

Tom patted him on the shoulder reassuringly. 'Don't worry, I think you'll find this one is just up your street. What's more, I'll make it worth your while,' he added as an inducement.

Robert jumped up in protest, upsetting his drink again. 'I wouldn't dream of charging you, after everything you've done for the family.'

'Nonsense.' His host held up his hand. 'All I did was put in a word for your uncle at the right time, like anyone else would do in the circumstances. No, the job I have in mind will need a great deal of your time and effort, involving research and heaven knows what. And above all, it's highly confidential ... and extremely personal.' He broke off and blew his nose to hide his feelings. 'Look here, can I rely on you to keep the details to yourself?'

'Yes, of course,' agreed Robert, bewildered. 'What do you want me to do?'

Taking his question as acceptance, Tom Conway went on to explain, 'Quite simply, it's to find a missing person. To be accurate, the daughter of a dear friend of mine who meant so much to me,' he took a deep breath before he could continue,—'at a particularly low point in my life. Before we go any further,' he added, 'you'll need to take some notes. My memory's not so hot these days.' He tossed over a pad and Richard caught it automatically.

'It must have been over twenty or so years ago.' Tom thought back. 'I was in a good steady job that took me away from home a great deal, and that's where the trouble all started. To put it in a nutshell, my wife Sylvia got bored with me being away so much and fell under the spell of a neighbour of ours, Dick Willis, rot his boots. We'd been to school together and I'd always regarded him as my best friend.' He snorted. 'Fine friend he turned out to be. When I got back from one of my trips, I found they had both gone and all I had left was a note.'

'What happened?' Robert found himself asking.

'I went to pieces,' the other said simply. 'Took to drink and came home smashed every night. They didn't say anything at first in the office, thinking it might blow over but, in the end, I got the push. The only thing that saved me was the help and devotion of a nurse who lived next door. Sheila was her name – she was an angel in disguise, I'm telling you. If it wasn't for her, I'd have given up and kicked the bucket years ago.' He sighed. 'You can guess what followed. After a particularly boozy night, she helped me into bed and that's when it all began.'

'She comforted you?' Robert put it diplomatically.

'You could call it that, but it wasn't just a fling, as I found out. What began as a night of passion developed into a loving and caring relationship, something I will always remember.'

Detecting an ominous note in his last words, Robert ventured to ask, 'What put a stop to it?'

Tom sighed again. 'After I got the push, I tried my hand at writing, something I'd always wanted to do, but never thought it would come to anything. I managed to sell a story and thought I was there. Funnily enough, I ended up doing the same sort of stupid things all over again ... chasing after freelance jobs and writing articles for companies that meant being away and travelling all over the place. As a result, I was never at home when I was most needed, and you can guess what happened. Sheila found out she was pregnant before one of my trips overseas. I couldn't get back in time and she had the baby alone.' His voice shook. 'It was all too much for her and I was too late. She was gone and lost forever.'

'And the baby?'

'I never found out. When I got back, I was told the baby had been adopted and that was that.'

'Did you make enquiries? You mean you couldn't find out what happened to her?' Robert was shocked.

'You're darn right I couldn't.' The reply was full of bitterness. 'Apparently, being Irish, her family arranged for her to be taken in by some convent or other over there, or so they said, and I was never able to make out what happened.'

'Was it a boy or a girl?'

Tom Conway buried his head in his hands helplessly. 'All I can tell you was before I left on my last assignment, she was expecting a girl.'

'But-but surely her family would know something?'

'If they did, they wouldn't tell me.' His voice was savage in his despair. 'They blamed me for everything; it was like running into a brick wall.' Reacting to Robert's bewilderment, he relented. 'You must understand. I was earning practically nothing in those days, except for the clothes I literally stood up in. By the time I managed to put some money together, I must have spent a small fortune on some enquiry agency or other trying to find out. It used up just about every penny I had. But it was no good – they came back with the same answer every time. Vanished without a trace.'

Robert was mystified. 'What do you expect me to do about it?'

Conway studied him earnestly. 'Listen, you're my last hope. I want you to find out the truth, whatever it costs.' He added sadly, 'I'm well provided for these days, so money is no object. If you take it on you can use this study as your base, no problem.'

'What about your family? Won't that prove a little difficult?' asked Robert tactfully, thinking of the mercifully absent Brenda.

For an answer, his host lost no time and dashed out a note and handed it over. 'There you are – if anyone asks, you can show them this. I will also sign a separate letter, stating the purpose of the assignment is to locate the whereabouts of my missing daughter, but that should only be revealed in the strictest confidence. Will that do?'

The statement was short and to the point. Robert studied it and repeated the contents out aloud. 'To whom it may concern. I, Tom Conway, authorise the bearer, Robert Bruce, to have unrestricted access and full use of my study to carry out a personal assignment at my request, whenever he requires to do so. Signed, etc. ... More than enough,' agreed Robert, well satisfied.

His host wrote the second letter and handed it to Robert, then coughed. 'No need to go into any reasons at this stage, is there, particularly with that nosy sister of mine? All she wants me to do is to buy some swanky holiday place in the south of France, so she can spend all my money for me.' He grumbled, 'Seems to think I've got nothing else better to do, when all I want is to finish off that last chapter of a book I'm stuck on. Now that you're here, it'll be a load off my shoulders.' He opened a drawer and pulled out a wad of notes and peeled off a fistful. 'Here you are. Is that enough to go on with?'

Robert blinked at the sight. 'Here - wait a minute! I can't take all that.'

'Go on, don't argue, you can always pay me back anything that's left over. But I've got a feeling that you'll need a hell of a lot more than that before you've finished.

'Good Lord, is that the time? Off you go and get some

beauty sleep. Give my regards to your uncle when you see him.' As he opened the door to wave goodbye he added, 'By the way, you might remember to drop in that tomato ketchup of mine sometime. Can't wait to tuck into my fish and chips again.'

But in this event, his wish was to remain unfulfilled, as Robert was to discover.

As the door closed behind him, Robert checked his watch before setting off. Ten o'clock, too late now to call in to see that old lady in the High Street, the next one on his list in need of help. It could wait until tomorrow. He couldn't wait to tell Uncle Ted about his good fortune and see the expression on his face. Perhaps it would stop him going on about that boring old solicitor's job. The thought of it made him yawn. Pulling himself together, he decided it was time he went to bed and caught up on some sleep. *It's been a long day and a lot to think about*, he reflected. *First a bath to freshen up, then a quiet drink to celebrate.*

But when he got back to his digs, he found it was not so easy as he had thought. The drink was there, but apparently there was some trouble with the bath. Luckily, the landlady's son, Brent, came to the rescue and found there was a blockage in the pipes.

'He'll soon fix that for you,' beamed his proud mum, surveying the tools spread out on the floor. 'That's nothing after some of the repairs he has to sort out down at the garage; you wouldn't believe. While he's doing that, come downstairs and I'll knock you up a sandwich while you're waiting.'

It was eleven o'clock by the kitchen clock when Brent was satisfied and gathered up his tools. 'Try it now, sir,' he suggested, straightening up. 'I think you'll find that's okay. Here, I'll run it off, you'll see.' Waving aside Robert's grateful tip, he grinned. 'Makes a change from some of the smash-ups I see to.'

So, Robert got his bath, a steaming hot one, and he wallowed happily in it before rinsing off and thankfully climbing into bed.

Before drifting off. his mind went back, remembering all the good times their two families had enjoyed together and the unfailing generosity of Tom Conway, his uncle's friend over the years. How he had stepped in to offer help when Dad was ill and had to take early retirement. 'He was like a second father to me,' he murmured. 'The least I can do is to pay back some of his kindness.'

The next day, there was a new spring in his step as he washed and shaved. Picking up Tom's letters and the notes he'd taken about his assignment, he set off to call on his Uncle Edward and break the good news.

Halfway there, he checked his stride as his memory caught up on him. *Ketchup.* He knew there was something he'd clean forgotten about – his promise to Tom. He mustn't forget that. Changing direction, he called in at the Home Stores to remedy the situation. Armed with his purchase, he made his way to Rose Lodge and blithely knocked on the door, ready to hand it in.

After a few minutes, he knocked again, slightly surprised at the lack of response. He looked at his watch. Half past nine, somebody should be up by now. Before he could follow it up, the door opened cautiously and Jill, Tom's secretary, stood there clinging to the frame, tears streaming down her face.

His smile vanished. 'What's wrong?'

Without thinking, she threw herself into his arms sobbing. 'It's Tom – he's dead!'

2

ONE OR TWO THINGS

'Pull yourself together,' he remonstrated gently in shocked disbelief, patting her on the shoulder, his heart racing at the unexpected warmth. 'Who told you that? He was perfectly okay when I left him last night.'

'You'd better come and see.' She pulled away and stood back, slightly embarrassed at the close contact, and tried to wipe away her tears.

He followed her into the study and was struck dumb at the sight that met his eyes. His old friend Tom Conway was lying back at an unnatural angle in his armchair, with a gun in his hand and traces of dried blood that had been oozing from his head.

'See? He's left a note,' she breathed behind him.

Careful not to touch anything, he edged around the desk and peered over his late friend's shoulder. 'It's no use, I must put a stop to it ...' he read aloud. Looking up, he blurted out. 'But this is nonsense – it can't be suicide! When I left him last night, all he wanted to do was to finish off that last chapter of his latest book ... and look,' he pointed at the smudged manuscript lying on the desk, 'he was only halfway through a sentence, nowhere near the end. He wouldn't have left it like that, knowing how long he takes to get it right, and he's stone cold. Besides,' he added, puzzled, 'it's all wrong. The gun's in his right hand and he's *left-handed*.'

'You've noticed that too,' Jill whispered faintly, agreeing with him.

They looked at each other.

'Someone must have done it,' she said at last, voicing their thoughts.

'Has anyone told the police?' Robert did his best to be practical as he stood there helplessly, trying to come to terms with the shattering loss.

'I rang Doctor Meridew as soon as I found Tom, to see what he thought.' A bell rang in the distance. She shivered and instinctively clung to him for support. 'That'll be him now.'

Reluctantly letting go of her, he straightened up. 'We'd better let him in. Look here,' he said awkwardly, 'would you like me to handle this? You look all in.'

'No.' She was positive and nestled closer. 'I was the one to find him, so they'll want to ask me all sorts of questions and I can't face it alone, so don't leave me, please Robert.'

'Don't worry,' he promised, trying to sound reassuring. 'I'm not going anywhere.' He would have enjoyed prolonging the contact but, putting his feelings aside, he eased her away reluctantly. 'You'd better answer it.'

As soon as the door was opened Doctor Meridew bustled in, taking charge in his usual hearty manner, which helped to relax the tension. 'Where is he?' Seeing the state Jill was in, he glanced kindly at them both. 'Why don't you both go and sit down somewhere while I take a look? I'll let you know directly.'

Robert accepted his brisk advice gratefully and ushered Jill into the adjacent morning room. After a brief pause, while Jill stared into the distance twisting her handkerchief forlornly, Robert did his best to take her mind off it.

'Is his sister Brenda at home?'

Jill came to with a start. 'Sorry, I was miles away, I still can't believe it's happened.' In answer to his question, she concentrated with effort. 'I don't think she can be; she would have heard something by now.' Thinking aloud, she recalled, 'The last time we spoke, she was going to a show last night with her husband, and I think she was going to stay over with some friends. Tom would know ...' Realising what she had just said, she mumbled miserably, 'I'd better go and see.'

Left to himself, Robert went over the events again in his mind, striving to make sense of it all whilst grieving over his old friend's death. If he didn't shoot himself, who could have done it and what was the motive? His speculations were interrupted by the sudden return of the doctor, who came straight to the point.

'He's dead all right, poor devil ... looks like suicide, on the face of it. Damned odd though, the whole thing.' He became lost in thought.

Robert interrupted his musing. 'Do we have any idea when it happened?'

'Eh? Oh, I would say sometime last night, between ten and midnight. Certainly not any later.'

'What?' Robert couldn't take it in. 'Why that must have been soon after I'd gone. I left just after ten – if only I'd stayed a bit longer.'

The doctor shared his distress. 'I know, he was a fine man, don't blame yourself. It could have happened anytime if his mind was set on it. He had a dicky heart as well, you know, which didn't help. Mind you, there were one or two things that don't add up – odd that.' Before Robert could express his own misgivings, he glanced at his watch. 'Forgive me, I must be off. Got another urgent patient call. Give my apologies to Miss Jill and pass on my condolences if you would. By the way, I've phoned the police with the details – it'll all be in my report.'

The front doorbell rang.

'That sounds like him now. Goodbye, let me see, Robert, isn't it?'

'Yes, Robert Bruce,' he added automatically. 'But wait, what did you mean?'

'Sorry, must dash, take it up with the inspector,' he advised and, not wasting any more time, he was gone.

But it wasn't the inspector, it turned out to be the friendly presence of Sergeant Lark, a well-known face in the village.

'Good morning, sir. Inspector Platt will be along shortly, he's got held up on another case. Meanwhile, if you could show me where it happened, I'll make sure nothing's been tampered with, if you get my meaning.'

Robert stirred himself with effort. 'Of course, it was Miss Gates who found Tom – I mean, Mr Conway. She'll be down in a few minutes.'

'Thankee. Mr Bruce be it, or should I say, Robert the Bruce? My wife's told me all about you, sir.' Then remembering where he was, he put on a suitably sad expression. 'Fine upstanding man, that. A great loss, to be sure.'

Robert coughed. 'Right, well I'd better show you where it happened.' He led the way to the study and, wiping his face at the incongruous sight that was all that remained of his old friend, he left the sergeant in charge.

In contrast, the chief inspector when he came, wasted no time in preliminaries. 'Evening, sir. Where's the body?' he demanded curtly. 'Just show me the way. I take it Lark's here?'

He marched in the direction Robert indicated, without further ado.

When Jill returned, she found him nursing a glass of beer in the kitchen, with a frustrated look on his face. 'Has the doctor been?' she asked anxiously. 'What did he say?'

Slapping down the glass, Robert said bitterly, 'Treated it as a suicide, what d'you think? Oh, and there were "one or two things" that don't add up. I ask you, it's staring you in the face.'

'Not if he didn't know Tom was left-handed,' said Jill out of loyalty to the doctor. 'Did he call the police?'

'Yes, and I bet that man Platt will say the same thing, by the look of him. He's in there now.'

Before he could comment any more, the door behind them opened and the Inspector re-appeared, barking orders over his shoulder, as he did so. '...and tell that photographer I want the usual kind of shots; he'll know what I mean. Ah, there you are, Miss Gates? I understand you discovered the deceased – what time was that?'

'Nine o'clock this morning,' she answered obediently. 'The clock in the kitchen had just struck.'

'And you, sir. Robert Bruce, am I correct?' He ticked off his list.

'Yes, but I must tell you ...'

'Just answer my questions if you don't mind. I understand you were the last person to see him before it happened? What time was that?'

'About ten o'clock last night. But—'

'All in good time, sir. What sort of spirits was he in? Depressed and anxious, was he?'

'No, on the contrary, he was full of good spirits.'

'Typical. Not wanting to show his true feelings. I expect.'

'But that's not what happened.' Robert felt his anger growing, despite himself. 'He was asking me to do something for him. It was about—'

'Usual thing in these suicide cases,' the inspector interrupted curtly. 'Only natural. He wanted everything to be sorted out before he took the final step. It's all in the note he left. "I'm going to put a stop to it", he says. Tells the whole story.'

'But you've got it all wrong,' cried Robert heatedly. 'You don't understand.'

'You'll have your chance at the inquest,' retorted Inspector Platt shortly. 'Providing it's relevant. I've seen the doctor's report. As I see it, it's a simple open-and-shut case. And a note to go with it, what more do you want? That reminds me.' He shouted, 'Lark, where are you, dammit? Ah, there you are,' as the sergeant's head appeared at the door. 'Directly the photographer's got what he wants, call the ambulance and don't forget to lock the door afterwards and clear the scene. We don't want any locals around gawping.'

He picked up his hat. 'Good night to you, miss, and you, sir, and if you don't mind, see that nobody goes near the study, particularly any nosy reporters sniffing around – not that they'll find anything of interest.' And with those dismissive words of wisdom, he strode to the door and left.

'What an officious man!' exclaimed Jill feelingly. 'He wouldn't listen to a word you said.'

'Not one of nature's sparkling gems,' agreed Robert abstractedly. 'I'll just have to wait until the inquest now, I suppose. More to the point, how are you going to manage? I can't leave you all alone after what's happened.' He glanced apologetically at the closed study door.

'I've got to stay here in case his sister calls. But you don't need to wait.' She smiled nervously. 'Ronald rang while you were with the doctor. He's promised to come and look after things.' She pressed his arm impulsively. 'I'm so glad you were here though – I don't know what I'd have done without you.'

'Don't give it another thought.' His face fell at the mention of her boyfriend. 'In that case, I'd better be off and let Uncle know – he was a great friend of Tom's.'

'I know,' her voice trembled. 'He was my best friend too.' As he moved to the front door, she called after him. 'You are as well, don't forget.'

~

It was with a heavy heart that Robert approached his uncle's modest bungalow in a little avenue set back off the High Street. It took a long while for anyone to answer and, when at last the door opened, Robert knew the news had got there before him.

His Uncle Edward stood there dabbing his eyes and nursing a glass of whisky. 'The postman's been,' was all he said, trying to mask his grief. 'Come on in.'

Robert followed his uncle into the small front sitting room and sat facing him, while his shaken relative helped himself to a handful of tissues and mopped his face.

'Tell me all about it.'

Taking a deep breath, Robert did as he was told, relating everything that had happened, from the moment he had delivered Tom's order the day before up to the shocked discovery of his old friend's death the next morning, and the unhelpful attitude of the inspector.

'Typical,' was the sarcastic response when his uncle heard about the inspector's reaction. He threw his wet tissues in the wastepaper basket in disgust. 'How he ever managed to get where he is today, I shall never know. He's a right Pratt and always has been.'

'Platt,' Robert corrected him automatically.

'I was right the first time,' his uncle fumed. 'If I told you some of the things he's been up to over the years, you'd never believe me.' He paused. 'So, Tom was left-handed, was he? I don't remember that. I should have known.'

'Yes, he was holding a drink in his left hand the whole evening I was there.'

'I can't wait till you tell them that at the inquest,' said his uncle grimly. 'How is he going to explain that away? Suicide, indeed. He'll look a right twit trying to put that one over.'

'I'm not the only one who noticed. Jill, his secretary, spotted he had the gun in the wrong hand right away. She should know, if anyone.' Thinking over his uncle's previous remarks, he said impulsively, 'I've never asked, but why is it you never got on with Platt?'

Taking a swig of his unfinished whisky, his uncle replied succinctly, 'Jealousy, simple as that.'

'But I can't imagine anyone being jealous of you?' Robert was mystified.

Replacing his glass on the table, the other decided to explain. 'It all started with that murder case back in the 90s that hit all the headlines. You probably don't remember; it was before your time. I was just a sergeant then, helping our bright inspector solve an unexplained death of a well-known financier in the City. The man was loaded, and the sole beneficiary was his wife, a ravishing blond called Gloria, who our inspector promptly fell for, hook line and sinker.'

'So, what did he ask you to do?' asked Robert, scenting a story.

'He wanted me to find any sort of evidence that would clear her as a suspect.' He shrugged. 'He was besotted.'

'And did you?'

'What I did find,' chuckled his uncle with relish, 'was a load of poison she had stashed away that would have been enough to kill off a herd of elephants.'

'That didn't please him, I take it?'

'Please him? He was livid until he found out she was having it off with a toy boy on the quiet.'

'So, did he thank you for getting him out of a hole?'

'Did he, heck. He changed his tune after that and claimed the credit for the whole bang shoot. I didn't even get a mention. How do you think he got his promotion?'

'But didn't they find out he was trying to get her off? Didn't it all come out at the trial?'

'What trial?' his uncle quizzed him ironically. 'Someone tipped her off and she did a runner, only to end up in a multiple pile-up on the motorway.'

Robert digested this. 'That should have satisfied him. All neatly tied up and forgotten about.'

'You'd think so. The trouble is, he seemed to think it was all my fault and blocked any hope I had of any promotion after that. If it wasn't for dear old Tom, bless his heart, I would have rotted away until my retirement.'

'Do you mean Tom Conway? How did he help?' Robert was intrigued.

'By the time all this happened he was making quite a name for himself with his writing and was able to pull a few strings on my behalf. I don't know how he did it, but he was able to get me transferred to a new patch where I got a promotion and was eventually able to retire as a respected member of the force, thank goodness.'

'Good for him,' Robert exclaimed warmly. 'He always struck me as a kind hearted type. Someone you could always rely on to help out when it's most needed.'

His uncle regarded him affectionally. 'You don't know it, but you have every reason to be grateful. You might as well know now, although he swore me to secrecy on the subject at the time.'

'About what?' Robert's curiosity was aroused.

'Did it never occur to you how your father managed to get you privately educated, as well as landing that promising position with those solicitors of his?'

'No.' Robert was bewildered. 'I always thought he must have inherited something. Otherwise, how ...?'

Uncle Ted decided to reveal the long-held family secret. 'It was all paid for by Tom, out of his own pocket, that's how.'

'What?'

'That would explain a lot of things,' mused his uncle aloud. 'Tom told me all about his life turning upside down when his wife ran off with that so-called best friend of his. And being saved from thoughts of suicide by an angel of a nurse who came to his rescue in the nick of time.' He pondered for several seconds. 'I don't think he ever got over that business of her dying and the awful business of what happened to the baby afterwards. You see, he told me he'd always wanted to have a boy to take after him and when that didn't turn up trumps, he pinned all his hopes on discovering the whereabouts of the girl, and that never happened. Which is why, in a way, he invested in your future as a kind of father figure, I suppose.'

'I see,' said Robert slowly. 'I've got an awful lot to thank him for ... and now,' he added bitterly, 'I shall never be able to repay the debt.'

'Don't worry, my boy,' said his uncle kindly. 'I'm sure if he could hear our conversation and the way you feel, he'd understand.'

'I hope you're right,' said Robert thickly. 'If it's the last thing I do, I promise you I'll find the murderous swine that did this to him. And I'll do my damnedest to find that little girl of his, I swear I will.'

His uncle patted him on the shoulder. 'I'm sure you will, knowing you. Mind you, I should think she must be grown up quite a bit by now. How time flies.' He stirred. 'That reminds me, I'm expecting a call from another of my old friends, Reggie Mayfield, sometime today. He phoned to say he'd look in after hearing about Tom. We go back a long way, to our days in Hendon together. I must introduce you when he arrives. That idiot Platt will have to watch his step where he's concerned, if he's got any sense.' He chuckled. 'He doesn't know it yet, but my friend Reggie is our new chief constable.'

The words had no sooner left his lips when the front bell rang. 'That'll be him now, I wouldn't mind betting.' He heaved himself to his feet. 'You wait here, I won't be a tick.'

Robert remained where he was as he heard the front door open and the exclamations of mingled surprise and pleasure that took place in the hallway. Then the door was flung open and his uncle ushered in a smiling thickset man, sporting a beard.

'Reggie, allow me to introduce my nephew, Robert Bruce.'

'How d'you do?' The handshake was cordial and the voice brisk and friendly. 'I hear from Ted you were the last one to spend an evening with my old friend Tom Conway, before the tragic event took place. Suicide, I hear.' He shook his head. 'I find that difficult to believe. He was so full of life and had so much to offer.'

'Suicide, my foot,' retorted Uncle Edward. 'You want to hear what my Robert has to say about it.'

'Really? Tell me about it. I thought it had been established to everyone's satisfaction.'

'Don't you believe it. They've got it all wrong, by all accounts. While he's doing that, I'll get some drinks,' encouraged his uncle. 'Sit yourself down.'

'Cheers,' responded the chief constable, 'just what I need. Now then, Robert, don't spare the details, tell me in your own words. What makes you think it wasn't suicide?'

Won over by the warmth of the invitation, Robert wasted no more time and got down to it, going over the events once again, interrupted now and then by some shrewd questions from their visitor, until he had finished and the drinks arrived.

'Well,' summed up the chief constable, 'that's a remarkable young man you've got there, Ted. Brief and to the point and not a single aspect overlooked, as far as I can gather. He'd make an excellent detective. Just what we need by the sound of it. Sounds as if our man Platt's got it all wrong. Didn't you tell him what you'd found out?'

'That's not what I call him,' interrupted Uncle Ted darkly, and Robert followed up with some feeling. 'He wouldn't listen to anything I tried to tell him.'

'Yes, well we all have our "off days",' the chief constable said tactfully. 'I wonder what the good doctor meant by his remark that "there were one or two things that didn't add up"?' He turned to Robert. 'Did he explain why he said that?'

'No, he had another urgent patient he needed to see right away. He said he'd leave a report for the inspector.'

'I suppose it will all come out at the inquest.' He stroked his beard thoughtfully. 'Meanwhile, I must be careful what I say, seeing I'm here in my official capacity. Can't be seen to be interfering in the case in any way. It's a great pity. Now if it was only someone like your young nephew involved, I'd feel we were getting somewhere.'

'I know.' Uncle Ted choked on his drink at a sudden thought. 'Why don't you rope him in as a special consultant or something.'

'No, I can't see that working,' their visitor dismissed the idea regretfully. 'He needs some sort of authority, I'm afraid.' He picked up Robert's short note of authority from Tom Conway. 'This might be acceptable to the family, but I very much doubt to the inspector. It would have to be something more formal to back it up.'

'I have an idea.' Uncle Ted sprang to his feet in his excitement. 'I believe I might have the very thing.' He started rummaging around in an old box in the corner and produced a card triumphantly. 'What about this then?'

The chief constable studied the card doubtfully. 'What's this? The "What's your problem enquiry agency"? I can't quite make it out.' He turned the card over and read "Recognised and accepted by authorities and embassies worldwide." Where did you get this?'

'It was the agency Tom used when he was searching for news of his daughter all those years ago. I remember, he showed it to me. Would that do the trick?'

His old friend meditated for a moment, then his face cleared. 'D'you know, it might be just what we need, by George.

Although,' he rubbed his chin thoughtfully, 'he'd have to be called on to investigate the case at someone's request.'

'What's wrong with me, then?' Uncle Edward enthused. 'If anyone asks, I'm safeguarding my nephew's interests. That man's got no authority over me anymore, thank goodness. Even old Platt couldn't turn up his nose at this, eh Robert, my boy?' Seeing the unspoken doubt on his nephew's face, he added cheerfully, 'Don't worry, I'll square it with the agency. They'll be only too pleased with all the publicity it'll give them.'

'If I were you, I'd keep it in reserve in case that letter of authority from Conway doesn't work out. Meanwhile, I'll do all I can to help – unofficially that is,' beamed the chief constable. 'I'd better be off to Headquarters and find out the arrangements for the inquest. When that's sorted out, what about meeting up at my club, Ted my old friend? We've got a lot of catching up to do.'

3

IN HIS LEFT HAND

As he climbed the stairs to his digs, feeling a trifle more reassured at the thought that he now had the backing of the chief constable in his fight to get to the truth, Robert was halted by a shout from his landlady.

'Mr Bruce!'

Looking down over the bannisters, he called out, 'What's up, Mrs P? Didn't you get the note with my rent to say I was out?'

'It's not that, love. A Miss Gates wants you to ring. Ever so anxious, she was.'

Trying to disguise a sudden lift in his spirits, he replied as casually as he could, 'When was that?'

'A good hour ago – very urgent, she says.'

'Did she leave a number?'

'I've got it here somewhere. Wait a minute – here you are, love.'

He retraced his steps and took the note handed up to him. 'Thanks.' With slightly trembling fingers, he opened the message and read the number. He didn't need to write it down; it was etched in his memory from that moment on.

Back in his room, he picked up the phone and dialled her number. 'Jill, you rang. Is everything okay?'

'Oh, I'm so glad you answered. I've just been told there's an inquest on Saturday and they want me to be there. I can't get hold of Brenda or her husband, what am I to do?'

'Calm down,' he said soothingly. 'All they want to do is ask you a few simple questions about what happened ... nothing to worry about.'

'But I'm scared after that inspector said it was suicide. Even the doctor wasn't sure. Nobody will believe me. And Ronald says he doesn't think he'll be able to make it,' she added apologetically.

'Why not? It's on a Saturday. Surely he'll be free if it's the weekend?'

There was a marked pause before she answered in a subdued voice, 'He said something urgent had come up, something to do with his by-election. Sounds as if he doesn't want to be mixed up in it.'

Robert refrained from saying what he really thought. 'Don't worry,' he said, trying to sound reassuring, 'I'll be there to back you up. After all, I was with him all evening the night before, don't forget. They're bound to ask me questions.'

'You promise?'

'Honest Indian,' he said solemnly. 'Where's it being held and what time, by the way?'

'In the local village schoolhouse, so it says here. Saturday at ten o'clock.'

'No problem. I'll probably get my summons tomorrow. Cheer up.'

'Oh, you don't know what a relief that is, knowing you'll be there.'

'Think nothing of it,' he said lightly. 'I'll sport you to lunch afterwards and we can compare notes.'

When Saturday dawned, he glanced out of the window to see it had already started raining, and by the time he left it had turned into a steady downpour, making him dash for the car and get the wipers going. Assuming the weather would have put a lot of people off, he pulled in at the schoolhouse, expecting to find plenty of parking space. Instead, he had to park some distance away and make another dash for shelter, to find the schoolhouse crammed with people, some standing patiently at the back of the hall. *I should have thought that would happen*, Robert marvelled to himself, remembering Tom's fame as a novelist as he fumbled for his invitation letter before being ushered to a reserved seat at the front.

Sinking into his seat, he just had time to catch a glimpse of Jill in the row behind as he stuffed his overcoat under his seat when the usher called out, 'Robert Bruce, please take the stand.'

Robert found himself addressed by Mr Alastair Bunning, the local magistrate, an imposing looking clerical figure wearing a stiff collar, who peered down at him with keen, penetrating eyes. The spectacle was so unnerving, he thought for a moment he was up before a judge, attired in all his finery.

'You are Robert Bruce?'

'Yes, my Lord,' answered Robert, without thinking.

A brief smile flitted across the magistrate's face.

'I doubt if I shall ever reach such an exalted rank in my lifetime,' he said, a remark that set off one or two subdued giggles in the rows behind. 'Now, Mr Bruce, I understand you were the last person to speak to the deceased before the tragic event took place. Perhaps you would be good enough to tell us in your own words the purpose of your visit? More importantly, what was the state of his mind at the time? Did he appear depressed, or in any way suicidal, as the inspector has suggested?'

'Not at all,' answered Robert as firmly as possible, looking around and repeating it to add emphasis to his words. 'He was in the best of spirits and invited me in for a drink. Then he asked how I was getting on and we talked over old times until it was quite late, and I had to leave. That would have been about ten o'clock.'

His remarks started off a buzz of interest that caused the magistrate to rap on his table for attention. 'Please remember where we are,' he pointed out courteously, leaving no doubt that he expected to be obeyed. 'I must have order while the proceedings are under way.' His words produced an instant hush. 'Pray continue, Mr Bruce. Do you have any evidence to support your statement?'

'Yes, he asked me as a personal favour to undertake what he regarded as a particularly difficult assignment and was anxious that I would be able to provide answers as soon as possible. He couldn't wait to find out, he told me, he was so keen.'

'Did he indicate the nature of this ... assignment?'

Aware that the audience was waiting breathlessly, Robert felt inside his jacket and withdrew an envelope.

'I promised not to divulge any details as Mr Conway wanted to keep it confidential. But he wrote this letter...,' he passed it up for inspection, 'inviting me to make full use of his study, whilst carrying out my investigation.'

'This is quite remarkable,' commented the magistrate, reading the statement carefully. 'I am most indebted to you. It would seem to shed an entirely new light on the matter. Have you anything to add that may have some bearing on the evidence we have already received? I'm told he left a note stating, "I'm going to put a stop to it". Doesn't that suggest to you that he might have been harbouring thoughts of suicide?'

'No, I understand his sister was urging him to invest in a holiday house in France and he didn't agree with it. That was what I understood was the meaning expressed in that letter. All he wanted to do was to be left alone to finish his book.'

'I see. Is there anything else you can think of that might support your theory?'

Waiting for the excited babble to die down, Robert said with conviction, 'Only that, in my opinion, it couldn't possibly be suicide.'

There was a renewed buzz of interest, quelled by a warning glance from the magistrate. 'Ah, and what makes you so sure?'

The silence that followed was so intense that anyone could have heard a pin drop.

'Well, as I said, Tom, I mean Mr Conway, was anxious to finish off the last chapter of his book as soon as I left. He was having problems with the ending, he told me. And yet when I found him the next morning, he had given up halfway through a sentence.'

'One moment, Mr Bruce. Is it not a known fact that authors find themselves faced at times by what I understand is called "writer's block"? And are we not forgetting the theory advanced by previous witnesses that he was probably feeling depressed and emotionally disturbed at his inability to overcome the problem, which could, in some instances give rise to suicidal tendencies, I imagine.'

Accepting the fact reluctantly, Robert decided to play his last card that he hoped would settle the matter. 'With the Court's permission, I would like to ask a question. I understand that when my friend Tom Conway was discovered, he was holding a gun in his right hand?'

The magistrate checked the report in front of him. 'That is correct. Do you have any reason to doubt the evidence of the doctor who carried out his examination?'

'No, I'm sure he reported what he found to be the case.'

'Well then?'

Robert cast a quick look around to make sure he had everyone's full attention, then said simply, 'In that case, it couldn't have been suicide. He was left-handed.'

His words were almost drowned out by the reaction of the audience, as the significance of his remarks sank in. Raising his voice to be heard, Robert ploughed on doggedly. 'He had a drink in his left hand the whole evening, that's why I know for sure. Ask anyone in the family.'

There was a gasp in the background and the magistrate raised his hand for silence. 'Thank you, Mr. Bruce.' He cleared his throat. 'In view of this new evidence put before us, I will now ask Doctor Meridew to take the stand again to answer one or two further questions.'

A head bobbed up from the back and the familiar figure of the doctor appeared to take his seat again.

The magistrate shuffled his papers. 'Doctor Meridew, you have heard what the witness, Mr Bruce has just said, casting doubt as to the cause of death put forward by,' he was about to say 'the inspector' but tactfully re-phrased his remark, 'by the authorities', that the deceased committed suicide while the balance of his mind was disturbed. Have you anything to add to your previous statement? I understand you were inclined to accept that verdict.'

The good doctor gripped the rail squarely in both hands. 'It is quite true that after my initial examination, I was quite happy to accept the verdict that it was a case of suicide on the face of it, but if you remember I did point out that there were one or two things that didn't seem to add up.'

'Perhaps you would be good enough to share any misgivings you might have had with the court?'

The doctor turned to face the audience. 'The first thing that struck me was his unnatural posture. I mean, the way he sat there, holding the weapon in his hand. I have had the unfortunate experience of attending a number of cases of suicides before and the way he was holding the gun in his right hand didn't look right somehow. If we are to accept the view put forward by Mr Bruce, it all begins to make sense. If he was left-handed as has been suggested, there is no doubt in my mind that the bullet should have penetrated the other side of his head first, which was not the case, as the photographs taken at the scene will confirm.'

'Is that your considered view?'

The doctor nodded firmly. 'I have no doubt in my mind now that these new factors have come to light. It couldn't possibly be suicide. Now, if you'll excuse me,'—he glanced at his watch—'I have another urgent case to attend to.'

'Thank you, Doctor Meridew.' His dismissal was interrupted by a crash at the back of the court. He coughed. 'I think if you can spare the time on the way out, your services might be required by one of the witnesses who appears to be in some need of medical attention.'

Shuffling his papers together, he addressed the audience. 'Having heard the latest testimony, I do not propose to call any more witnesses under the circumstances. It is quite clear, from what we have just heard, that the deceased, Tom Conway, did not take his own life. The only possible verdict therefore is murder by person or persons unknown.'

In the rush to leave with the latest hot news, headed up by a group of reporters, Robert was hauling his coat out from under his seat when he caught sight of Jill waving her hand to attract his attention.

'Hi, over here!'

Acknowledging her signal, he made his way to the back of the hall where she was waiting.

'Isn't it great?' she greeted him excitedly. 'I don't have to give evidence after all.'

'What happened to Tom's sister and her husband? I didn't see either of them in court.'

'They didn't get back till late last night, something to do

with the trains running late. The police took statements off them but, as they were away when it happened, the magistrate decided there was no point in them attending. And Bates is in the same boat. He's awfully cut up about it ... thought the world of Tom.'

'I told you there was nothing to worry about, didn't I?' he reminded her, relieved to see she had got some of her spirits back.

'All thanks to you,' she replied gratefully. 'I could kiss you for that,' she added and proceeded to do so, flinging her arms around his neck.

As the sweet embrace ended, far too soon as far as Robert was concerned, he was immediately tempted to take her in his arms again and smother her with kisses but, remembering her boyfriend, stepped back awkwardly.

Jill smiled at him warmly, then noticing his restraint, asked him mischievously, 'Well, where's this lunch you promised me?'

'Of course,' he agreed. 'Where would you like to go?'

'Why don't we celebrate?' she said demurely. 'What about The Swan? They do a lovely steak there – Tom took me there once.' Then realising what she had just said, her face clouded over.

'Steak and chips, it is,' decided Robert quickly. Changing the subject, he asked, 'What was all that fuss about just now? The magistrate said someone had fainted.'

Jill started giggling and he had to shake her gently before she was able to pull herself together. 'It was that inspector,' she managed weakly. 'He was so upset at the magistrate's verdict, I thought he was going to burst a blood vessel or something. You should have heard him; he was *livid*.'

'But why?' Robert was mystified.

'Because he'd already convinced them that it was suicide. He's now doing his best to blame it all on *you*.'

'But the doctor agreed with me once he knew the facts.'

'You don't know Platt. It's his pride. Once he's made up his mind about something, he can't stand anyone arguing about it. You've made him look a complete idiot with that verdict.'

'Can't help that, I'm only interested in getting to the truth,' said Robert soberly. 'I'll find out who that murderous swine is if it's the last thing I do.'

'I know.' She touched his arm in sympathy. 'Tell me about it over lunch.'

Later, in the cosy elegance of the restaurant, Robert found himself relaxing slightly.

Sensing the change in his manner, Jill took the plunge as her curiosity got the better of her. 'What's our next step then?' she asked lightly.

Taking her into his confidence, he began by bringing her up to date with his discovery that his friend Tom Conway had been his guardian angel, paying for all his school fees without his knowledge and swearing his Uncle Edward to secrecy over the whole matter. Then, to crown it all, the unexpected visit by the new chief constable, who turned out to be an old friend of his uncle and inspired him with new confidence about hunting the killer.

'Oh, how sweet, and you didn't know about it, all this time. How typical of Tom.' Seeing it was a time for confessions, she smiled at the memory. 'I must tell you, he came to my rescue just at the right time, as well.' Encouraged by his interest, she went on. 'I was on my beam ends at one point. I saw his advertisement looking for a secretary and turned up as a last resort, without any qualifications or references, and he took me on just like that.' She brushed away some tears. 'He was so kind, like a father I never had. I shall never forget.'

Robert patted her hand consolingly, not wishing to probe any further. 'I can well understand. That's just the sort of man he was.' To take her mind off the subject, he told her about the idea his uncle had of using an enquiry agency as a cover to help him carry out his investigations.

Forgetting her own sorrows for a moment, she greeted his news with excited admiration. 'How exciting! You make it sound like an Agatha Christie thriller. Do you think you'll get away with it? You know how suspicious that inspector is. He won't like anyone else taking the credit.'

Robert shrugged. 'I'll just have to wait and see.'

'Have you worked out who the prime suspects are?'

'Not yet,' he admitted. 'I was hoping you might be able to help me on that.'

'Let's face it. Unless it turns out to be a complete nutcase who we've never heard of, it's got be one of the family ... oh, not forgetting Bates, the gardener, I suppose.'

Robert frowned. 'I don't see how it can be him. He was going off to visit his cousin down with flu the day before when I was there and he's only just got back, so you were saying. In that case, we're left with his sister Brenda and her husband, Harold. From what I've heard about him, he wouldn't say boo to a goose, let alone kill anyone.'

'Pity it wasn't Brenda,' reflected Jill aloud. 'She's a right old tyrant. But I can't see how either of them could have done it. They were both away, staying with friends after going to that theatre on the night it happened, so that lets them out.'

'I take it they'll be hearing from the solicitor after the funeral?'

'She'll be off like a shot when she hears all right; she wouldn't miss an opportunity like that, with all that money in the offing,' declared Jill with feminine insight. 'All she's waiting for is to get her hand on the ready, so she can nip off to the south of France.'

'Yes, I remember him saying something about that,' said Robert, thinking about the note Tom left. 'All he wanted to do was to be left alone to finish of that chapter of his.'

'By the way,' she said suddenly, 'you've forgotten about one of the chief suspects.'

'Who's that?' he asked puzzled.

'Why me, of course.'

'Don't be silly.' He regarded her affectionately. 'You cared about him as much as I did … and still do,' he corrected himself.

'That doesn't mean you should rule me out,' she insisted. 'Look, Robert, I've got as good a motive as anyone else. How d'you know I wasn't madly jealous of all those lovely ladies who got to know him and were after his money?'

'I don't believe that for a moment,' he declared stoutly. 'Anyway, I know for fact there was only one woman he cared about in his life, and she seems to have disappeared without trace.'

'Oh, you mean that ex-wife of his, Sylvia, who ran off with his best friend?'

'No, I do not. That's something else I still have to follow up.'

'Oh, and who's that?' she asked scenting a mystery. 'Do tell.'

Robert hesitated for a moment; then, remembering how close she was to his old friend, decided to reveal his closely kept secret. 'There's not much to tell you at the moment,' he confessed, 'because Tom wanted to keep it confidential. But, apparently, when his wife ran off with his best friend, he went to pieces and the only thing that saved him was the help and devotion of a nurse next door called Sheila, who gave him all the love he needed and the will to live.'

'But it didn't stop there …' she prompted when he paused.

'No,' he agreed. 'It went too far and when he returned from one of his trips, he found she had given birth to a daughter, but she didn't live to see it. And that's who he asked me to trace.'

'How romantic …and yet how sad,' she reflected softly. 'And all these years, he's never known who his daughter was and what happened to her.'

'Anyway,' Robert continued, 'my first priority is to get on the tracks of this swine of a murderer.'

'How are you going to do that?' she enquired, trying to be practical. 'You're not going to get any help from Platt after the latest fiasco, and I can't see Brenda agreeing to anything. I know,' she whooped, struck by a sudden thought, 'why don't we team up together? We'd make a great partnership.'

'No,' was his immediate reaction. He was quite definite about that. Seeing her look of hurt disappointment, he softened. 'Look, it's not that I don't appreciate the offer, but you must realise it would be far too dangerous, as far as you're concerned. Once the murderer knows you're involved, your life would be in constant danger. And that's the last thing I want. I tell you what. Why don't you act as my silent partner? You could keep me informed, unofficially, of everything that's going on in the house. We could set up a system of keeping in touch. On the quiet.'

Jill agreed with a reluctant pout. 'What I still don't understand is how are you going to manage on your own? Have you got anyone to help you?'

'Don't worry about me,' he reassured her airily, hoping he would sound convincing. 'I'll get my mate Gus to give a hand. You know, the one who helps me with the deliveries. He's always hard up. I could engage him as my assistant. Now that we've got that sorted out,' he went on more cheerfully, 'how does that leave you? I expect there's still masses of things for you to do about Tom's work that will keep you hard at it for months to come.'

'I don't know about that,' admitted Jill candidly. 'Tom's agent will carry on, looking after the sales side, without any help from me. In fact, I wouldn't mind betting Tom's books will be in greater demand than ever. To be honest, I don't know what I shall do now. I expect I'll have to start looking for another job. Which reminds me, before you say anything, I've just received a letter from Tom's solicitor, a Mr Arbuthnot. He wants me to attend a meeting after the funeral for the reading of the will. What shall I do?' she asked anxiously.

'Calm down,' he said soothingly. 'I expect he wants you there to take a note of the meeting. That's probably it, nothing to worry about. You've been to these sort of meetings dozens of times before.'

'But you don't understand. He wants me there because he says I'm down as a beneficiary. What does that mean?' She started to panic.

'Why that's great,' he said encouragingly. 'It just goes to show how much he thought of you, after all the work you've done. It's only what you deserve.'

'But the whole family will be there. Please say you'll come and give me some support. Please.' Her voice started wobbling.

'Be reasonable,' he argued gently. 'I'm not one of the family. I've got no excuse to be there.'

'But you have,' she insisted. 'Didn't I tell you? You're down as one of the beneficiaries as well.'

Her news left him almost speechless. Thinking back, his natural instincts rebelled against the whole idea. He'd only agreed to accept Tom's proposal as far as he knew, nothing else. 'There must be some mistake,' he objected.

'Well, you must have done something,' she argued, 'otherwise you wouldn't have been invited. Haven't they told you? You *will* come and back me up though. Promise! I won't know what to say if you don't.'

'I'll be there,' he agreed, to put her mind at rest. 'What time is it?'

'Ten o'clock next Wednesday, after the funeral. I'm so glad you'll be there. Bless you.' She gave a big sigh of relief and pressed his arm before leaving.

~

Back at his digs, Robert sat staring at the phone for a moment, trying to make sense of it all, before ringing the solicitor to find out what it was all about.

'Mr Arbuthnot? Is that you, Henry? Sorry to bother you. Robert Bruce here. About this reading of Tom's will. I don't understand why you've got my name down as a beneficiary. Are you *sure* you want me to be there?'

There was a hint of exasperation in the solicitor's voice. 'Hasn't that secretary of mine let you know yet? Of course, I want you there, otherwise the whole thing will be a waste of time.'

'I've been out. Why me?' Robert was mystified.

'You'll see. Can't go into details right now, but make sure you turn up. Sorry, got another call waiting, can't wait. See you after the funeral. Don't forget. Bye.'

4

IT MUST BE THE HEAT

'What have we got so far on the Conway case?' enquired the new chief constable, Mayfield, as he entered the operations room later at Police Headquarters. 'Anything to report?'

Inspector Platt sprang to attention, full of self-importance. 'Nothing to get our teeth into so far, sir, but it looks promising. I've taken statements from the family and we're still checking them out. We'll have a better idea as to motive once the will is read out on Wednesday.'

'Hmm. Who's the chief suspect if we exclude any outside marauders?'

'Lark!' the inspector barked, making the chief constable wince at the outburst. 'Look lively. Where's the file? Here we are, sir. The nearest relative to the deceased is his sister, Brenda, sixty-eight, ex-schoolteacher, married to one Harold Williams, fifty-two, insurance clerk in the City. The talk is she's likely to inherit a tidy sum after death duties. Conway must have put by a small fortune over the years, judging by his book sales. If you remember, it came up in the inquest that she was trying to persuade him to buy a holiday house in the south of France and he was digging his heels in about it.'

'Right, let's check out her movements during the night in question. What about Harold, the husband? He's a lot younger, I see. Anything on him?'

'There is a suggestion in some quarters that he married her for money, sir, on the strength of her brother's connections. Apparently, he was involved in some minor fraud some years ago, but nothing was proved. He struck me as a very weak character, though. I wouldn't have thought he had it in him unless he paid someone to do it for him to give him an alibi.'

'Yes, there is that, I suppose. Well, keep digging. What happened to that wife of his? Sylvia, wasn't it? Didn't she run off with his best friend?'

'I wouldn't have thought he would have left anything to her in the circumstances, sir. A bit of a long shot. It may take some time to find out where she lives.'

'Follow it up. And this secretary of his, Jill Gates, I think she's called.'

'We don't appear to have any background information on her, sir. Everyone says she was devoted to the deceased. It seems her boyfriend is hoping to get elected into Parliament at the next by-election.' He rifled through the brief. 'Goes by the name of Ronald Chambers, I understand.'

'And the gardener, how does he fit in?'

'Another one devoted to the deceased, sir, and well thought of, according to the family. He had special permission to take time off to visit his cousin who was down with the flu at Longbridge, some ten miles away. He came back as soon as he could which, again, was well after the event took place.'

'So that's the lot, is it? Seems as if you've got a full house there.'

'Nothing out of the ordinary, sir. All in the day's work. But there is one individual I would like your advice on.'

'Really, who's that?'

'A young man who calls himself Robert Bruce, a friend of the family, so he says. Keeps interfering with our lines of enquiry, if you know what I mean.'

'No, I don't understand what you mean, Inspector. Enlighten me.'

'Well, sir. We were on the point of wrapping up the case to our satisfaction, when along he comes with all sorts of theories that turned the inquest into some kind of circus.

'Unfortunately, I can't pin anything on him,' he went on reluctantly. 'He left the deceased shortly after ten o'clock, and we have just received information that the deceased's agent,' he consulted his notes, 'a Mr Jeremy King, phoned the deceased at ten past ten on the evening in question, asking when he'd get the latest draft of his novel so he could start some advanced publicity. The call lasted about twenty minutes, sir, and the autopsy report just in puts the time of death about ten-thirty or thereabouts.

'According to his landlady, Bruce got back to his lodgings shortly after ten and it's only a short distance away down the High Street where he lodges. He had a witness to that effect. Apparently, there was some sort of blockage with the bath where he lodges and while the landlady's son – by the name of Brent – carried out the repairs, the landlady allegedly made him a sandwich, and chatted with him until about eleven,' his tone gave a hint of his disappointment, 'when the repair job was finished.'

'I see, well done. By the way, how can we be sure about the time of death?'

'The deceased suffered a heart attack; it's all here. He was known to have heart problems. The sight of the intruder with a gun was enough to set it off, I would have thought.'

'So, he could have died before he was shot, is that what

we're saying? That timing clears Bruce, then. Why the reservations? What have you got against him?'

'It's just his general attitude, sir. Very obstructive, I'd say. Wouldn't believe a word I told him.' He snorted indignantly. 'I'd like to keep an eye on him, with your permission, of course.'

'I don't quite follow your reasoning there, Platt. From what I've read about the case, I considered his contribution to be quite significant. If it hadn't been for him, the magistrate might have brought in a verdict of suicide, which would have been a most unfortunate error, to say the least.'

'If you say so, sir.' The inspector swallowed his disappointment with effort. 'You don't think I should regard his actions as unwarranted interference then?'

'On the contrary, Chief Inspector. I think you will find he will be able to offer a fresh insight in the unravelling of this case. You will come to thank him for it when it's all cleared up, I have no doubt. I'm sure you will come to appreciate any help he can give you.'

'I will, will I?' His words came out as a strangled grunt.

'Yes, I forgot to tell you. His uncle, Edward Bird, is an old friend of mine. We passed out as police cadets together. We go back a long way.'

'Indeed, sir,' he said heavily. 'I was not aware of that.'

'You look a bit off-colour, Platt. Don't overdo it, old chap. Well, I must be off. Keep me informed. Regular reports and all that. You know the drill. No, don't get up. I suggest you open his collar, Sergeant; he looks a bit faint. It must be the heat.'

Directly the chief constable had left, the inspector slammed the report shut. 'So that's all the help I can expect. Lark, where the devil are you? Listen, I want you to keep a close eye on that Bruce character. Let me know what he gets up to. Immediately, is that clear?' He repeated the chief constable's summing up scornfully. '"Most unfortunate error", was it? We'll see about that.'

As the day of the funeral approached, Jill went through all her clothes in the wardrobe in a hunt to find something suitable. In the end, she rang Robert in frustration. 'I can't find anything to wear. What shall I do?'

Robert cast his mind back to other similar family functions. 'The last one I was at, they all managed to find something black, or on the dark side. You're not the only one. I've only got an old office suit to wear.'

'Men,' she wailed, 'you're no help. It'll have to be the outfit I wore for my interview, I suppose. That's all I've got – at least I can still get into it.'

'Fine, you do that. I'm sure you'll outshine the rest of them. I'll pick you up about 9:30, shall I? We want to make sure of getting a seat.'

'Don't be silly,' she scolded. 'You'll never get anywhere near the church to park. The world and his wife will be there, don't forget. We'll walk. It's not that far.'

'Of course,' he accepted cheerfully. 'Make it quarter past nine and I'll bring an umbrella, just in case.'

'Do you think I'll do?' she appealed when she opened the door.

"You look gorgeous" was on the tip of his tongue, but he wisely refrained. 'You look fine,' he assured her.

'So, do you.' She smiled shyly. 'Look, I don't think it's going to rain. Why don't you leave that old umbrella behind, in the hall? We'll be coming back afterwards anyway, for the solicitor. The cook will give us a cup of tea; there's bound to be a crush after the service.'

When they reached the church, Robert had to admit that Jill had been quite right. The old weather-beaten walls of St.

Augusta no doubt had valiantly stood up to hundreds of years of onslaught by Norman invaders in the distant past, but faced with the funeral of a famous novelist, they gave in without a murmur. Today, the doors were opened wide for visitors who had queued up in the dozens to pay their respects. As a result, the entrance was full of a long line of patient fans and parishioners, all waiting to be admitted.

Robert was at the point of giving up when a familiar figure beckoned them in. It was Bates, the gardener, almost unrecognisable in his Sunday best. 'Sir and Miss, in here,' he gestured. Following him in with difficulty past the pressing throng, Bates explained in a whispered aside, 'Got a couple of seats reserved.' Accepting their thanks as they squeezed into their seats, he explained, 'My cousin got me to book a couple in case she could make it, but the doctor said she wasn't fit to travel yet.'

Robert murmured his condolences and Jill leaned across. 'I do hope she's getting better, Bates.'

'Thankee, Miss. She'll appreciate that, I'm sure.'

They were interrupted by the opening peal of the organ signalling the start of the service, and they sat back to join in what turned out to be a fitting tribute to a much-loved author.

As the vicar mounted the pulpit to begin his sermon, Jill whispered, 'There's Brenda and her husband in front.'

'She looks a bit overcome by it all,' murmured Robert sympathetically, as the sobs could be clearly heard above the measured tones of the reverend.

'Don't you believe it; she's putting it on,' retorted Jill scathingly. 'She's been practising that act of hers ever since she got up this morning. You wait till the solicitor starts reading the will. She'll turn off the tap soon enough when that happens, you'll see.'

And so it proved. When the time came, after they were all assembled in the dining room back at Rose Lodge where the table had been cleared for the occasion, the solicitor, Henry

Arbuthnot, handed over a large handkerchief that his secretary had provided for such an emergency, neatly folded in his top pocket. As soon as she heard his voice, Brenda sat back dry-eyed in her usual forbidding manner, all attention focussed on what they were about to hear.

'I should explain,' Henry Arbuthnot began, 'that part of this legacy is in the nature of a trust, a term which some of you may recognise or not, as the case may be.'

'I do, but I'm sure my wife won't,' interrupted Harold Williams coldly, anxious to get on. 'Kindly explain.'

'To put it in the most simplistic terms, it means that after certain bequests have been made, which I am about to disclose, a certain sum has been set aside in anticipation of an agreement that was subsequently reached between my client and his friend, Mr Robert Bruce, who I am glad to say, is present here today.'

Immediately, a row of heads swivelled around and focussed on an embarrassed Robert.

'What has he got to do with it, I would like to know,' demanded Brenda majestically.

'As soon as I have made you acquainted with the terms of the will, I am sure Mr Bruce will be able to satisfy your questions on the matter,' explained Mr Arbuthnot. 'Now, if I can have your attention, I will proceed.'

'Of all the nerve – fancy bringing in an outsider,' Brenda was heard to mutter to herself as she sat back firmly in her seat.

'Thank you.' The solicitor cleared his throat. 'This is the last will and testament of Thomas Conway, dated the eighth of June 2020.' He glanced up. 'I shall not bore you with the usual terminology, but I will endeavour to make it as simple as I can, if that is agreeable. Under the provisions of the will, there are several bequests outside the family. To James Bates, who is employed as my gardener, I leave £2,000 in view of his selfless attention looking after my garden in all the time he has been with me ...'

There was a stunned silence and he raised a hand to quell any dissent. 'And to Jill Gates, my devoted secretary, the sum of £30,000 ...'

This time there was a gasp of 'never!' from an outraged Brenda, supported dutifully by her husband, amidst murmured speculation.

'If I may be allowed to continue. Thank you. And now for the main provisions relating to the family. To my sister Brenda, I leave my house and the bulk of my estate, after other bequests and trusts have been paid out.'

Brenda preened and Harold started calculating to himself and hastily scribbled something in his notebook,

'Providing she gives an assurance that she no longer wishes to sell Rose Lodge and invest the proceeds into any property located outside our present county boundary.'

'*Wha-at*?' demanded Brenda fiercely. 'I'll see about that!'

Harold mouthed urgently to his wife as she was about to protest. 'We shall contest that. For goodness sakes, don't say anything now.' To his obvious relief, she subsided in her seat again, fanning herself furiously.

'Now, coming back to the provisions of the trust which I mentioned earlier,' reminded their solicitor, 'I will explain the main features. As I was saying, my client, as some of you know, has not always been as successful as he is today, or was, forgive me. Some twenty years ago, before he turned to writing, his wife, frequently upset by his unavoidable absences due to his work, decided to leave him.' He added diplomatically, 'For what purpose, I do not propose to dwell on here. In his resultant state of mind, he turned for comfort to a neighbour, a nurse who subsequently,' he paused delicately, 'bore him a daughter, so we understand, out of wedlock.'

'That's old history,' interrupted Brenda, affronted. 'What's that got to do with it?'

'I will explain if you will allow me,' said the solicitor,

remaining unruffled. 'Apparently, he spent years trying to discover the whereabouts of the child in question, without success, despite calling on the resources of a private enquiry agency, which is where our young friend, Robert Bruce, comes into the story.'

'What's *he* got to do with it?' objected his inquisitor, clearly upset and on the warpath.

'Perhaps I'd better explain,' interrupted Robert, feeling sorry for the solicitor. 'I was invited in for a drink after delivering his groceries on the day in question and he told me all about it.'

'A delivery man?' sniffed Brenda, wrinkling her nose, as if offended by a certain unmentionable smell.

Undeterred, Robert went on, 'Because I was able to offer some advice in the past, Mr Conway asked me to undertake a personal assignment – in short, to find out what happened to his missing child. He was most insistent that I should start on the investigation right away, without delay.'

'A likely story.'

'I thought this might happen,' sighed Robert. He reached inside his jacket and pulled out an envelope. 'Just in case there might be any objection in some quarters, Mr Conway wrote this letter, giving me full authority to act on his behalf and make full use of his study in the course of my investigation.'

'Full use of his study?' squealed Brenda, jumping up, outraged. 'He'll do *no* such thing – I'll see my solicitor about that!'

'If I may have your attention,' added Mr Arbuthnot, 'I should have mentioned that following the terms of the will, a sum of money has been set aside for this purpose. According to the will, whoever undertook the challenge would receive the sum of £3,000 to begin his investigation and a further amount of,' he paused, '£30,000,'—the silence was broken by a gasp of astonishment from the gathering—'at the end of twelve months, should he prove to be successful in his endeavours.'

It was all too much for Brenda. 'What!' she screeched. 'Over my dead body!' With a convulsive heave, as if she was about to keep to her promise, she struggled upright to express her pent-up fury, before swaying unsteadily and collapsing in a heap at their feet.

'Is she ... dead?' asked Mr Arbuthnot anxiously, mentally revising the will and getting ready to cross her off his list of beneficiaries.

'No,' replied her husband bleakly. *No such luck*, he thought, seeing his hopes of inheriting a fortune disappear as soon as she opened her eyes again weakly.

'Well, in that case, I'm very much afraid,' announced the solicitor hesitantly, casting a quick glance around him as he gathered up his papers, 'that in view of the present situation ... ahem ... I think it would be better if we convened the meeting again at a later date, when Mrs Williams feels more up to the occasion. There are still some outstanding matters to discuss, but I am sure they will await our ... ahem ... attention in the not-too-distant future.

'Please pass on my best wishes to the good lady when she recovers, and I hope she will be feeling better shortly. Perhaps you would get in touch with me to arrange a date as soon as you feel it to be convenient. You have my number, I believe. My secretary has all the relevant dates when I'm available. It only remains for me to say how sorry I am on the way it has turned out and hope all the remaining matters will soon be resolved. Good day to you.'

Taking advantage of the situation, Robert warmly thanked the solicitor for his efforts and decided to seek out Jill, who had disappeared, and find out if she was all right, after all the unwelcome interruptions. Calling out softly outside her door, he was rewarded by it opening slowly, revealing a distraught figure.

'Oh, Robert,' she cried, collapsing in his arms. 'I can't believe anyone could be so generous. What am I to do? It's all too much to take in.'

'Shh, not so loud. Look, I can't believe it either. Why don't you go to bed and get some sleep and we'll have another word about it in the morning? Don't worry, everything is going to be all right, you'll see. Trust me.'

Jill gazed up at him mistily. 'I don't know, I can't think straight anymore.' She tiptoed up and brushed his cheek. 'Bless you, I don't know what I'd do without you. I'll ring you tomorrow.' Stepping back, she softly closed the door.

Robert woke with a start next morning as the telephone started ringing again. With an effort, he propped himself up and focussed his eyes on the bedside clock. 'Nine o'clock.' He had overslept. 'Who's that?' he managed drowsily.

'Robert?'

'Oh, it's you, Jill. What's up?'

'Wake up, lazybones. D'you know what the time is?'

'Sorry, I was late getting to bed. I was trying to get hold of Gus.'

'I thought I'd warn you and bring you up to date. Your friend Platt has been on to Brenda and is coming to see her at ten o'clock this morning to ask her a load of questions.'

'Where she was at the time, you mean?' He caught on. 'Not surprising, she had a strong motive on the face of it, with all that money he left her.' Feeling protective, he urged, 'Listen, when can I see you, this business of the will needs talking over.'

'You mean, he'll also want to know where I was that night in case I haven't got an alibi.'

'Not quite like that,' he mumbled defensively. 'But you know what he's like.'

She laughed. 'Only too well. Okay, you win. Meet me at the little café in the High Street, you know the one, in ten minutes.'

'Hang on, I haven't even shaved yet.'

'I don't suppose anyone will notice,' she joked. 'All right, make it twenty. I'll have a cup of coffee waiting for you; that should wake you up.'

Watch it, we're already beginning to sound like an old married couple, he thought inconsequentially as he flung on some clothes in a mad dash to escape before his landlady waylaid him and sat him down to a 'proper breakfast', as she put it. But what Jill told him when he arrived out of breath put all such romantic notions out of his head.

'I've got a confession to make,' she began in a rush, before he'd had a chance to sip his coffee. 'Ronald and I were … staying in a hotel together, the night it happened.' Seeing the disbelief in his face, she added quickly, 'Nothing like that, it was all perfectly above board. But if it all came out, Ronald says it would be the end of his political career. He begged me not to tell the inspector … he said it would ruin him.'

'I dare say it might,' Robert commented dryly. He forced himself to ask, 'Do you want to tell me about it?'

She buried her face in her hands. 'It's not what you think. He just asked me to meet up with him for a drink. He'd been to a party conference and, while he was there, he was asked to cover up for a politician, a friend of the family who'd got into some sort of trouble, so he said, and he wanted me to swear I was with them both at the time, staying at this hotel.'

'Sounds a bit fishy to me, Jill. What made you agree to such a mad idea?'

'I suppose I felt sorry for him,' she confessed apologetically. 'All he wanted me to do was to sign the hotel register with him.

He said it would put him in the clear. If it wasn't for that maid …'

'What sort of scrape had he got into?' he asked bluntly, cutting her short.

'Drugs, I think. Something like that.'

'You mean, you're not sure? You do realise that if the inspector suspects you are not telling the truth, you could be accused of something far worse?'

'I know.' She crumbled. 'Oh, Robert, what am I to do?'

Putting his feelings aside, he urged her strongly to refuse, sadly acknowledging the fact that by doing so, he was about to lose the friendship of the only girl he'd ever set his heart on. 'I know what I would do. I would ring up that boyfriend of yours and tell him to get lost. He's not worth it.

'Listen, as far as the inspector is concerned, all you have to do is to confirm you were staying at that hotel at the same time. He's only got to examine the hotel register to prove it. But as for the rest of it, it's all eyewash. I would ring him up and tell him. He can't force you. Otherwise, you could end up in the dock for something far worse.'

Jill took it all in and smiled somewhat ruefully. 'I thought you'd say that. You're quite right, of course.' She delved in her sling bag and pulling out her smartphone, started dialling. 'Hello, is that you, Ronald? I'm sorry if you're busy, but this can't wait.' She drew in her breath. 'Remember that favour you asked me? Well, the answer is "no", I'm afraid.' There was an outbreak of spluttering noises at the other end. 'I'm sorry, but what you ask is impossible. I don't care what it means. Do you want me to get arrested for murder?' She put the phone down abruptly, cutting off the cries of anguish at the other end.

Jill looked up and smiled sadly. 'You were right about Ronald, as well. He's not worth it.'

Reaching out impulsively, Robert did his best to cheer her up. 'It may not make sense at this moment,' he said, comforting her, 'but when this is all over and you find someone you can really trust, you'll be able to put it all down to experience.'

Jill looked at him queerly. 'I wonder who that might be. Heavens,' she said glancing at her watch, 'I must fly. That inspector will be sending out a search party if I'm not careful. Thank you for those kind words, I'll let you know how I get on.' And she was gone, leaving a faint smell of a floral scent lingering behind her.

5

A LIFELINE

'… And you were absolutely right about that awful inspector as well,' Jill began directly he lifted the receiver next morning, carrying on as if they were still where they left off the previous afternoon. 'Do you know, when I spoke to him on the phone this morning, he refused to accept a word I said? He's coming over later to get me to make a statement, he says.'

'I could have told you that.' He massaged his ear to ease the impact of her mounting indignation. 'D'you know what the time is?'

'Yes, it's time someone told that Platt where to get off.'

'Steady on,' he cautioned. 'He is the police, after all.' He checked his watch. 'Give me half an hour and I'll be right over. Meanwhile, don't do anything rash. It's about time I found out if that letter of Tom's is as good as he said it would be.'

Cutting himself a hasty sandwich and bolting down a scalding cup of coffee, he sneaked out, hoping his departure would not be noticed. Arriving at Rose Lodge, he felt in his pocket to make sure the letter was still there and knocked on the door.

Directly he saw the look on the cook's face, he knew he was not welcome.

'Oh dear, I'm ever so sorry, sir, believe me,' she stammered. 'Missus said I was on no account to let you in.' She glanced back nervously and whispered, 'Go round the back and I'll tell you about it.'

'No,' Robert silenced her with a reassuring gesture, 'don't worry, Rose, leave it to me. I'll take care of it.' He raised his voice. 'Please tell your mistress that Mr Bruce is here and wishes to speak to her.'

As he expected, the door behind her flew open on cue and a furious face appeared. 'Who the devil is that, at this hour? Oh, it's you, I should have known.' She regarded him balefully. 'What the blazes do you want. I gave strict instructions ...'

'Now don't go blaming Rose,' he admonished her reprovingly. 'She said all the right things, I assure you. Rose,' he repeated, considering the coincidence courteously, 'how apt, don't you think? Name of the house, and all that. Charming girl, I would have thought she deserves some help, now that things are looking up.'

Mrs Brenda Williams bristled at the suggestion. 'That's none of your business, young man. What impudence. How dare you tell me what I should do in my own house! Get out, this instant.'

'Tut, tut,' he soothed, catching sight of an official looking car drawing up outside, 'is that the way to greet the inspector? Is your husband handy, Mrs W? If so, I think you might be in need of some support.'

'No, he's at work, where you should be.' She broke off, putting on a fixed smile of welcome for the newcomer. 'Inspector, what can I do for you? Do come in. Mr Bruce is just leaving.'

True to his character, Inspector Platt wasted no time in getting down to the business in hand, pointedly ignoring

Robert. 'Mrs Williams, I have here your statement that you were away visiting the theatre with your husband on the night in question. Is that correct?'

'Yes, we hired a chauffeur from the local garage,' she answered haughtily, 'otherwise it meant relying on the train. Noisy smelling things. We couldn't have that, could we?'

'So, you went to see a show. May I ask, what was it called?'

'Yes, now what was it, don't rush me. Give me time to think.' Seeing his impatience rising, she gave in. 'That was the original idea of course,' she stalled, 'but my husband couldn't make up his mind, there were so many to choose from. I did so want to go, but ...' She flapped her hands helplessly, beginning to get flustered.

'But, what?' he snapped. 'Come now. Either you did, or you didn't.'

'Well, you see, that was our original intention, but ...'

The inspector stopped her coldly. 'I know, you just said that. Please do not waste my time, Mrs Williams. You realise this is a murder enquiry.'

'Yes, of course.' She became flustered. 'Now I remember ... we found that there was a mistake with the booking when it came down to it, so we didn't actually go.'

'So, what did you do?' he wanted to know.

'Do? I see what you mean. Well, the truth is ... we ended up with some old friends of ours, who gave us dinner and so on. So good of them at such short notice, don't you think? We weren't expecting it, or anything. They dropped everything to fit us in.'

'What did you do with these friends, after you had dinner?' he asked impatiently.

'Oh, I see what you mean,' she prevaricated. 'We sort of sat around chatting most of the evening, as you would expect. You know, chatting and so on and ... don't rush me, Inspector, my nerves are all on edge. You've no idea ... I think it must be the weather or something.'

'Excuse me, Inspector,' interrupted Robert, aware that she was playing for time, 'can't you see Mrs Williams is not in a fit state to answer your questions just at the moment?' He stood by, ready to forget her previous animosity as her obvious distress became apparent.

Accepting the lifeline blindly, she started wringing her hands hopelessly. 'If only my husband was here, he'd be able to tell you. They were his friends, you see.'

'Who were?' demanded the inspector, losing the thread.

'Daphne and Terry, I keep telling you. Our friends ... we've known them for ages.'

'And what exactly were you doing with these "old friends" between ten pm and midnight?'

A frown creased her brow. 'Let me see. That's right, we were playing cards,' she decided at last, somewhat reluctantly, 'that's what we were doing. My friends and the two of us.'

He sighed. 'Why didn't you tell me that in the first place? I must ask you, Mrs Williams, to come along to HQ as soon as possible to sign a fresh statement. My sergeant will tell you where that is. While you're at it, it's essential that we have the names and addresses of the friends you were talking about for confirmation, as well. Meanwhile, I need to talk to Miss Gates; is she here?'

Robert stepped forward. 'She's in her room, I expect. I'll fetch her if you like.'

'Thank you, Mr Bruce, I don't need you to help me,' he said stiffly, 'if you don't mind.'

'Right ho, I'll just be in the study. Just say the word if I can be of any help.' He flourished Tom's letter confidently in explanation. 'I expect you know all about this. Tom, I mean Mr Conway, suggested I use his study while I carry out my investigations.'

'Just a minute,' said the inspector sharply, annoyed at the freedom of movement Robert appeared to be enjoying. 'Has anyone given you permission to use that facility ... Mrs Williams?'

But Brenda was too full of her own problems to object without her husband there to back her up and merely nodded impatiently in agreement, leaving the inspector to ruffle through his papers, frustrated at the way his authority was being undermined.

He was about to explode when Jill, appearing from upstairs, drew comfort from the unexpected sight of Robert popping his head through the study doorway.

'You wished to see me, Inspector?' she asked nervously.

'Yes, Miss.' Irritated by Robert's presence, the inspector went through his now familiar routine, quoting her remarks from his report. 'About your movements on the night in question: it says here you booked in at the Kings Arms at 6 pm, is that correct?'

'Yes.' She nodded briefly, waiting for the inevitable follow-up.

'In company with your friend, Ronald Chambers?'

Again, she nodded in agreement.

'Can you account for your movements for the rest of that evening? For instance, did you stay the night alone or did you have ... company?'

She lifted her chin and nodded defiantly. 'Yes, quite alone, I assure you, Inspector. We occupied separate rooms.'

'Do you have anyone who could confirm your version of events?'

She hesitated before explaining. 'If you must know, we had an argument, and I went to bed early with a headache.'

The inspector pounced on her statement. 'Then why does your friend,' he consulted his report, 'insist categorically that you both stayed up late, discussing politics with a friend of his, before spending the rest of the night together?'

'That's not true,' she denied indignantly, stung by the accusation. 'He's making it up, to protect his friend's ... activities.'

'And those were?' the inspector barked.

Jill decided she'd had enough, and it was time to own up, regardless of the consequences. 'It's no use; you'll find out sooner or later, I suppose. The truth is, they were both into drugs, and Ronnie asked me to cover up for them, otherwise he said he would be ruined.'

'A prospective MP – he said that? Are you certain? Have you any way of,' he tripped over the words, 'substantiating this kind of allegation?'

'No', she admitted candidly.

The inspector sighed heavily. 'Then I'm afraid I must ask you to accompany me down to the station to put it all in writing. I feel it my duty to warn you under the circumstances, that everything you say at this stage ...'

'Wait!' cried out Robert impulsively, overhearing. 'Jill, *think*! There must be something you can think of that backs up your statement. Didn't you say something about a maid who served you that evening?'

Pressing a hand to her head, she tried to concentrate. 'Wait ... now I come to think of it.' She straightened up suddenly in recollection. 'It was after I had this awful headache and went to bed.'

'What time was that?' demanded Robert quickly.

'About nine. That's right, because I asked the maid to bring me something to help me get to sleep, otherwise I would have been awake for hours. I remember now, I looked at my watch to make sure – the maid will tell you.'

'There you are,' cried Robert, 'that's it, eh Inspector? In that case, she's in the clear.'

'If what you say is correct,' acknowledged the policeman, putting his notebook away reluctantly, 'you have nothing to worry about, Miss Gates. Thank you for your assistance, sir,' he added unwillingly. 'Let me see, that just leaves Bates to see. Well, that shouldn't be too difficult.' He sighed in resignation, realising he was not getting very far in resolving the case. 'I gather he went off to look after his cousin when she went down with flu. I'll get Lark to follow that one up.'

Long after the inspector had gone, they were still talking it over happily together. 'Thank you so much for being here,' breathed Jill, overcome by the close shave. 'I'd never have remembered that in all the confusion after the tales they were telling me. What made you think about it?'

'It was just something you said at the time about the maid. I'm glad we've got that all sorted out. Tell me, Jill,' he asked curiously, 'what are you going to do with that little windfall of yours, now you've got that all settled? Have you thought about it at all?'

'Why do you want to know?' she returned playfully.

'Sheer nosiness, I suppose,' he answered with a smile. 'Here you were, seems like only yesterday, you were all steamed up, wondering what was to become of you without Tom to look after you, and now look at you – a prize that any man worth his salt would give his half a kingdom to own.'

'But I don't want to be "owned", as you put it, dear Robert; you should know that by now.'

'I know, forget that I said it – you know what I mean, though.'

'Well,' she said demurely, 'nobody's asked me yet.' Before he could answer, she admitted honestly, 'At the moment, I've no idea what's awaiting me in the crystal ball. I expect I'll have a lot of catch-up work to do before dear Tom's affairs can be straightened out. Beyond that, I haven't a clue. What about you?'

He said simply, 'I owe so much to Tom for all the amazing things he's done for me and Uncle Ted all my life, which I've only recently discovered, and I'm just beginning to come to terms with it. I can't begin to explain what it means to me – it has literally transformed my life. All I know is, my priority at the moment is to find out what kind of devil it was who did this to Tom and make sure he is punished – if it's the last thing I do.'

'I know.' She pressed his arm, understanding. 'If there's anything I can do to help in any way, you only have to ask.' As he gazed unseeing into the distance, she bought him gently back to earth. 'And the other thing he wanted you to do?'

'Well,' he said doubtfully, 'even if I can't find the daughter, I'm certain he will be united together again with his sweetheart, wherever they are. That's what he wanted.' After losing himself in the thought, he apologised and got back to his more immediate priorities. 'However, my main aim at the moment is to discover the monster responsible.'

'And what if you're successful?' she asked gently.

He shook his head wearily. 'It's not going to be easy, but I'll get there.'

'What then? Will you continue the search for his daughter?'

'That's my second priority,' he agreed, 'not that there's much chance of finding out what's happened to her now, after all this time.'

'Meanwhile,' she persevered, 'isn't there someone out there waiting for you to ask the magic question?'

He smiled awkwardly, not looking at her. 'I'm afraid that's out of the question at the moment,' he said, sadly aware of the gulf that had opened up between them since the news of her inheritance. 'I can't afford to think about anything like that at present.'

'Not even with the prospect of all that money coming to you?' she teased.

He roused himself with effort and tried to be practical. 'That's all a tantalising pipe dream as far as I'm concerned right now.' He pulled himself together. 'At the moment, there is something that puzzles me about this business, if only I could remember what it is.'

'Come on,' she rallied, refusing to give up. 'Don't be morbid. What about that celebration? I'm dying for a drink, after all that.'

'I know what it was,' he remembered suddenly. 'Why was Brenda so keen to make us think they were playing cards when the inspector was grilling her? Brent would know; he works in that garage where they hired the car. I'll give him a buzz.' He lifted the receiver and dialled. 'Mrs P? Is Brent there, by any chance? Can I have a word with him? Thanks.' He heard his friend being connected after a pause. 'Hi, another early day? What d'you mean, your day off?' He chuckled at the answer. 'Listen, can you do me a favour? Did someone at your place take a Mrs Williams and her husband to the theatre recently? You did, did you? Tell me about it.'

At the end of the conversation he put down the receiver, slightly bemused at what he'd heard.

'Well?' enquired Jill, hiding a yawn. 'What was all that about? Don't keep it all to yourself.'

'Only that they didn't go to the theatre after all,' he revealed, sobered by the news.

'We know all that. Tell us something we don't know.'

'For a start, she was telling the truth when she said she was playing cards with Daphne – but it wasn't at home.'

'Where was it then?'

'Get this,' cried Robert, astonished by what he'd just heard. 'He ended up taking them to a ... you'll never guess, not in a million years.'

'Don't keep us in the dark, you beast,' said Jill, throwing a cushion playfully at him.

'To a gambling club, that's what!'

'Never – you're joking. Not that high and mighty Brenda – that paragon of virtue? I don't believe it.'

'It's a fact. According to Brent, they've been at it for years. They're both born gamblers and they've lost a packet over it apparently. Well, Brenda has, he doesn't know about Harold – too cautious by half, I expect.'

'I don't believe it,' she spluttered indignantly. 'After going on at me about not wasting money on things like bus fares and stationery and the cost of stamps, ever since I've been here, and all the time she's been losing it all on gambling, I ask you.'

'I bet that inheritance came along in the nick of time,' observed Robert soberly. 'If they haven't already spent it. That's a thought. I wonder how she's getting on with that inspector?'

As they suspected, the interview was not going too well for Brenda Williams, who was protesting loudly at the way the inspector's questioning was heading and demanded to see her lawyer.

'You are perfectly within your rights to see your lawyer,' agreed the inspector stolidly, 'but wouldn't it save a lot of time and effort if we could agree on the details of your movements on the night in question?'

Sensing the net was closing in around her, Brenda was beginning to panic. 'I refuse to answer any more questions until I speak to my lawyer,' was all she would say.

'As you wish,' accepted the long-suffering inspector. Lark, have you managed to contact him yet?'

'Not yet,' was the harassed response.

'Are you going to keep me here all night?' demanded Brenda, expecting an answer. She sniffed. 'Ask anyone where I was – even that man Robert Bruce believed me.'

The chief constable, who was present, pricked up his ears at her chance remark and intervened. 'We don't seem to be getting anywhere at this point, Platt. I think you'd better let the lady go for the moment. Meanwhile, I'll have a word with Bruce and see what he has to say.'

'As you wish, sir,' sulked Platt. 'You are at liberty to go, madame, for the moment. But we might well need to interview you again, before long.'

'In that case, just make sure my lawyer is present,' was the defiant reply and she stalked out of the room, slamming the door behind her.

Directly she was gone, the chief constable picked up the phone. 'Put me through to a Mr Robert Bruce, will you, operator? I have the number. Yes, Rose Lodge.' Within minutes he was deep in conversation with his young friend, who was able to give him all the information he needed.

At the end of their discussion, he put down the phone with great satisfaction. 'You'll be interested to hear that the lady in question was in fact playing cards as she stated, Platt. But what she omitted to inform you was that she was playing for high stakes. It turns out that in certain circles she is well known for her insatiable gambling habits, as a result of which she is heavily in debt. Bruce has managed to get hold of the driver, who took her to a notorious gambling den where she was a frequent visitor. He works at the local garage, name of Brent, by the way. Bruce can vouch for him – he's just come back with all the evidence we need.'

Platt's jaw dropped. 'A well-known gambler? Then we've got her,' he exclaimed excitedly.

'She says she was playing there all evening. Anyway, that's her alibi. You didn't ask the right questions, it seems.'

'Never mind that, sir,' Platt asserted stubbornly. 'If she was heavily in debt, as you say, that makes her a prime suspect in our murder case.'

'If that's true, it's another good reason why you should thank Robert Bruce for finding that out.'

But Inspector Platt was not listening. 'You heard that, Lark.

Get her in for questioning again. And while you're at it, have a word with that witness at the garage, Brent he calls himself, and check out her story – and don't let him out of your sight.' He rubbed his hands gleefully. 'This time we'll find out what she was *really* up to that night.'

6

SOMEONE TO RELY ON

It was a weary Brenda Williams who alighted from a taxi on her return and went straight to her bedroom, clutching a large gin.

An hour later, feeling marginally refreshed, she tottered downstairs and ordered the cook to prepare a light snack to revive her spirits. After that, feeling in a condescending mood, she summoned Robert and expressed her lofty thanks in her usual majestic manner and ended dismissively, 'Tell the cook I'll be in my room if anyone needs me. I feel quite faint after that cross examination by that dreadful inspector.'

Surprised at her unexpected approach, Robert made a dutiful response before she swept away in search of a top-up and to make another futile attempt at contacting her solicitor.

Left to review the situation, he pondered over his next move. If he was going to get anywhere in his investigation, he would need some help from someone he could trust. The question was, who? What he needed was someone who was free to make enquiries on his behalf at the drop of a hat and, more importantly, someone he could rely on who was reasonably intelligent. Gus was the name that immediately sprang to mind, but thinking it over, he hesitated. Most of his friend's time lately seemed to be focussed on clocking up overtime for Home Stores, when he wasn't chasing new girlfriends. No.

As he was toying with the problem, a picture of Brent presented itself. Why not? It was worth a try. He could only say no. He debated whether to discuss the idea with Jill first, but then decided to leave it until the whole arrangement was settled. He didn't want her involved at this stage of the enquiry – it would be far too dangerous. If the murderer felt threatened, he reasoned, who knew what he might do to protect his identity. He hoped and prayed it might be a 'he'; he had no stomach for unmasking a possible female assassin.

It turned out that Brent was only too willing to oblige when he phoned.

'We've got so little work coming in at the moment, the Guv's had to cut down and lay us off for a couple of weeks until things get better,' he explained. 'So, what d'you want me to do?'

Robert wasted no time. 'You remember you told me about Brenda Williams and her trip to that gambling den? I want to find out how long she stayed there that night and who we can get hold of to prove it.'

'When do we start?'

'Good man. Just give me a few minutes while I fill Jill in, and I'll be with you. Can you lay your hand on some transport, by the way?'

'Sure, my old banger's sitting there doing nothing. I just need to fill up before we start.'

'Right, come and pick me up in about five minutes and I'll be ready.'

It turned out that Jill had her own ideas on the subject. Staring at her face in the mirror, she wondered for the umpteenth time what she could do to get Robert interested. Couldn't the fathead know how she felt about him? She knew instinctively why he was so shy in expressing his feelings. One didn't need to be a nuclear scientist to work that one out. Ever since that family solicitor of theirs had announced that amazing bit of news about her inheritance, she'd been aware of a sudden gulf that had sprung up between them. Although she respected his feelings on the subject, there must be something she could do to make him see sense. She combed her unruly locks until she was satisfied they would pass inspection and prayed for inspiration.

After his hesitant knock on her bedroom door and hearing about his friendship with Brent, the answer came to her out of the blue. She would go with them and start the ball rolling. It was an ideal opportunity to make him jealous. Hopefully, that might spur him on. *Now's my chance*, she thought, giving him a sweet smile.

'What a great idea,' she enthused, 'when do we start?'

Turning the idea down with his usual apologetic excuses, he said firmly, 'No, it might be dangerous. Why don't you stay behind and look after Brenda?'

'She's fast asleep,' Jill retorted swiftly. 'She doesn't need looking after.'

'Look, it's for your own good.' *And my peace of mind*. 'It might be dangerous, mixing with all those gamblers. I'd much rather you stayed here, where I know you'll be safe.'

'Why wouldn't I be safe with two strong men to look after me. Besides,' she argued, 'I'd be worried all the time you're away. Please let me come – I'll be quiet as a mouse, promise.'

'All right,' he agreed reluctantly. 'Make sure you are.' They were interrupted by the sound of a car's toot outside. 'That sounds like him; we'd better be off.'

Jill was off like a shot and Robert was about to follow when there was a knock at the door and Bates, the gardener, approached him deferentially, cap in hand, with a guarded expression. 'S'cuse me, master Robert, can you spare a moment?

'Of course. How can I help?'

The gardener coughed discreetly. 'Be that Mister Brent I see outside, sir?'

'Yes, I believe so, why?'

'It's just that, well ... they do say he be the one that drove Mistress Williams to that there gambling place.' He shuffled his feet in embarrassment. 'I know it's not my place to say like, but I'm told there's a rumour going around he's in with a bad lot. That's what they say in the village anyway. I thought you ought to know about it. Hope you don't mind me mentioning it.'

'No, of course. It's the first I've heard about it.' Robert was taken aback. 'He seems a decent enough sort to me – he's my landlady's boy, you know. But thanks for telling me. I'll keep my eyes open, now you've mentioned it.'

'I'm much obliged, sir.' He gazed at Robert earnestly. 'I hope you don't think I'm speaking out of turn. I only want to make sure nothing else is likely to bring harm to the family, after what happened to the master like.' His eyes moistened at the thought. 'I thought the world of him. I don't care who knows it. He treated me like a gentleman, bless him.'

'I can imagine, Bates. Don't worry, I'll watch my step. Is everything okay otherwise in the garden?'

'Fair to middling, sir, thank you. The roses are giving a spot of trouble, but I'll soon put that right. They just need to know who's boss, that's my way of thinking. Any trouble from them and I'll get my old weed killer out.'

Robert dismissed him and went to find the others, musing over what he'd just been told. Much as he respected Bate's warning, he couldn't believe there was any substance in it. Mrs P would have soon let him know if there was. After turning the idea over in his mind, he dismissed it as idle gossip and went in search of Jill.

He was delighted to find that she was of the same opinion. If anything, she took to his friend like a duck to water. He was gratified to see that she put on her best behaviour as she was being introduced to Brent before climbing into the back seat. In fact, once they got going and the conversation loosened up, he couldn't help noticing that she seemed very attracted to her new friend – in fact, it dawned on him she was being far more attentive than he thought necessary, much to his chagrin.

'Oh, do tell me about your work in that garage of yours,' she urged, leaning forward. 'It must be terribly interesting.'

Feeling slightly disconcerted at becoming the focus of attention, Brent said self-deprecatingly, 'Not really. I just do all the odd jobs, giving the old bangers the once-over now and then and a lick and a polish.'

'Now you're being too modest. I'm sure it's not like that at all.'

'Don't embarrass the poor chap,' Robert called over his shoulder from the front seat, mildly censoring, 'you'll put him off his driving. He'll have us in the ditch if you don't look out.'

'No danger of that,' laughed Brent. 'But keep an eye on the road someone, I seem to remember we turn off somewhere along here, if I remember rightly.' True to his word, a junction warning appeared, and Brent slowed up, peering at the sign-post ahead. 'This looks like it. We're nearly there.'

Half a mile along the road, he pointed to a turn-off on their left. After a hundred yards or so, another sign appeared announcing the entrance to their destination, with a gaudy sign reading 'Harry's Bar'.

Getting out of the car, Brent warned, 'I should be careful if I were you. There's some funny looking characters on the door acting as bouncers, if I remember from last time.'

Smoothing out her skirt, and satisfied that she got things started in the right direction and had given Robert something to think about, Jill asked, 'Who's going to lead the way? Do we need a password to get in?'

'Leave it to me,' advised Brent in an undertone. He strode to the entrance, raising a friendly hand in greeting as he was about to enter.

'Half a mo,' challenged the bouncer. 'Who said you could go in?'

'They all know me inside.' Brent assumed a confident air. 'Mrs Williams knows who we are. We're friends of hers.'

'Here, Jeb – is that right?' He turned to ask the other for verification.

'Yus, she was here last week, Mat. It's okay, let them in.'

Mat eyed them dubiously. 'Don't look like the usual sort of regulars to me.'

Seizing the opportunity, Jill decided to intervene. She stepped forward, waving a bulging wallet in front of his nose enticingly. 'Would this help?'

The bouncer's eyes nearly popped out of their sockets. 'That'll do nicely, ma'am,' he said weakly, stepping aside.

'Don't forget, we want the top table,' she commanded. Her bold air of assurance raised her standing to a new level in Robert's eyes as she had hoped, and she swept in confidently, leaving the others to follow.

In the ensuing exchange of mutual congratulations, nobody noticed a small dark saloon slip through the entrance and park quietly in a space at the back where the driver could keep a close eye on the proceedings. As he sat there unobserved, the headlamps of a passing car lit up the driver's face, revealing the dogged features of Sergeant Lark.

Inside, the atmosphere had an unhealthy air of feverish anticipation, mingled with the stale smell of cigarettes and cheap perfume.

Tipped off by the guards at the entrance, the manager came oozing up to them, anxious to please.

'Can I be of help, Madam and Messiers?'

'We're looking for a friend,' explained Robert, scanning the room and slightly at a loss, not knowing where to start his search.

'What name shall I say?'

Turning to Brent, Robert said hopefully. 'My friend here might know. What did you say her name was?'

Never at a loss, Brent answered promptly, 'Daphne, a friend of Mrs Williams.'

The manager's face cleared. 'Ah, my good friend, Mrs Williams. Why didn't you say? If you would step into my office, I will make enquiries.'

As he ushered them in, Jill marvelled at the lush interior. 'Goodness, what a lovely room ... and just look at those pictures,' she breathed as an aside, 'they must be worth a fortune.'

Overhearing, the manager beamed modestly. 'Just a few items some of my clients insisted on donating in return for a small favour or two,' he said, hurriedly sweeping a pile of IOUs into a drawer. Hastening to put the record straight and present himself in a more favourable light, he brushed a non-existent tear away from the corner of his eye and declared manfully, 'I mustn't bore you with my own petty problems and the struggles I've been through to get where I am.'

He struck a pose in front of a picture and peeped out of the corner of his eye to see if his words were having an effect. 'If my dear mama was alive, she would be able to bear witness to all the heartaches I've suffered to make my little business the success it is today. Not now,' he hissed as an anxious assistant appeared at the door with a pile of complaints in her hands. Suddenly remembering where he was, he straightened up apologetically. 'Forgive me, you were about to let me know how I can help you.'

'Mrs Williams's friend, Daphne,' prompted Brent quickly, before the other could resume his life story.

'Ah my good friend, Daphne ... er, Smith,' he said smoothly, pressing a bell. 'Patrick,' he said as a face appeared, 'do you know where we can find, Daphne, um, Smith?'

'Oh, the old boozer, you mean?' the waiter replied without thinking, then seeing they had visitors, repeated hastily, 'Oh, *that* Daphne Smith, she's in the Loo ... the Lieutenant's Room. I'll go and see if she's,'—he was about to say 'fit enough' and quickly re-phrased his remarks to—'free ... to see visitors.' He wiped his brow and disappeared.

'There you are,' offered the manager quickly. 'I'm glad we've got that sorted out.' Not to lose out on any opportunity that presented itself, he opened a drawer and produced a box full of chips.

'While we're waiting, perhaps you might care to try your luck on the tables, with a throw of the dice.' Seeing them hesitate, he urged, 'No, it's on the house, I insist.'

'Come on, what are we waiting for?' asked Jill breezily, putting into words what they were all thinking. Without waiting, she made the decision for them by helping herself to a handful.

'*Faites vos jeux, messieurs et mesdames*,' invited a sad-eyed croupier at a nearby table.

Putting on a brave face, she slapped the whole lot on the nearest number without a second's thought and waited excitedly.

'*Faites vos jeux, messieurs et mesdames*,' repeated the croupier. After one or two more tipsters strolled over and finished placing their bets, the croupier called out mechanically, '*Rien ne vas plus*!'

'What does that mean?' whispered Jill nervously.

'No more bets,' explained Robert, looking on apprehensively, waiting for the croupier to rake in her chips, signalling the end of her hopes.

After an agonising few seconds, the wheel stopped spinning and the croupier called out crisply, '*Vingt et un*!'

Jill waited breathlessly, expecting the croupier to gather in her lost bet. Instead, to her astonished delight, the man pushed a heap of chips in her direction.

'Does that mean I've won something?' she asked disbelievingly.

Robert gathered them up and handed them over, secretly amused at her success. 'Don't look now, but I think you've just hit the jackpot.'

'You lucky girl. Game for another flutter?' asked Brent enviously.

'Not on your life,' Jill decided. 'I know when to quit. Let's go and celebrate.'

'I think you've earned it,' was the agreed verdict.

Sinking into a seat by the bar, Jill sipped her drink gratefully. 'I could do with that. My nerves are shattered. I wonder what Brenda would say. She'd be green with envy.'

'Speaking of which,' interrupted Brent suddenly, 'I think I'll have a word with that lady over there who's just come in, if you'll excuse me.'

Jill craned her neck. 'I wonder who that is?'

Observing the two of them in close and animated conversation, Robert was reminded of the warning Bates made earlier and it set off a faint alarm bell in his head. 'No idea,' he admitted, eyeing them curiously. Before he could add anything further, he saw Brent urge his companion to get up and join them. He noticed the woman seemed to stagger slightly with the effort, but finally made it to their table.

'May I present, Daphne – an old friend of Brenda's,' Brent added meaningly to the others. 'Daphne, allow me to introduce my friends, Robert Bruce and Jill Gates.'

Catching on, Robert jumped to his feet, instantly forgetting his suspicions, and welcomed her warmly, not believing their luck. 'How do you do? Brenda has told me so much about you.'

Daphne swayed as she groped for a seat and sat down with

a thump. 'Any friend of Brenda's s'is a friend of mine,' she slurred.

After touching lightly on some current topics of conversation, Robert did his best to steer the subject around to Brenda's recent visit. 'I'm sorry to hear she didn't manage to get to that theatre, after all.'

'Is that what she told you?' She banged her glass pointedly on the table. 'Wanna nother drink.'

'Of course.' Robert jumped up quickly. 'Waiter! Another round please.'

Gulping down half the contents in one go, she hiccupped, 'That's what she told you, was it?' She smirked. 'Believe that and you'll believe anything.'

'So, where did she really go?' appealed Jill winningly. 'You can tell us, can't you – just between friends?'

Answering to a nod from Robert, Brent left the table and returned with a bottle of Scotch wrapped discreetly in foil. Clasping it fondly before tucking it into her voluminous handbag, she gazed around craftily and winked. 'That would be telling, wouldn't it, my dears?'

Brent disappeared again and returned with an expensive looking bottle of perfume.

'Ta deary, my favourite. Well, as I was saying, that's what she told the rozzers, but we know differently, don't we?' She sat there, drawing on a limp cigarette. 'Don't think much of these fags either. Got a light?'

Without a word, Brent got up and had a word with the barman and brought back a box of miniature cigars to add to her collection.

'Go on, you're spoiling me. Now, where was I?' She gazed at them owlishly, fuddled by all the drink. 'If you really want the truth, she was up to her usual tricks – gambling, of course. Right up to midnight was it, she told 'em? Her and that shrimp of a husband of hers. But we know differently, don't we, darlings?' she leered. 'Between you and me, I can tell you what she was doing. Had an alibi, did she? Blow that for a lark. If you really want to know, she spent all her time ranting on about that brother of hers and what she'd like to do with him, all because he wouldn't divi up and buy that swanky holiday place she'd set her heart on. Threatened to kill him, she did, and that's the truth.

'And all in the space of an 'our or so. That's right,' she pronounced with dramatic effect. 'Left here at eight o'clock sharpish, I remember looking at my watch. Said she had to get back for some reason or other.' Having got that off her chest, she sat back with a contented burp and slumped in her seat.

'Oh, my word,' exclaimed Jill, horrified at the story. 'That's done it. What do we do now?'

As if in answer to his question, a police whistle shrilled and Brent alerted them urgently, 'It's a police raid. Quick, out of the side entrance. Follow me, I know the way.'

After the excitement died down, a waiter crawled out from under a nearby table and shedding his disguise, Sergeant Lark patted his miniature tape recorder and stowed it away.

'You all heard what she said,' Robert reminded them when they got back to Rose Lodge. 'No wonder she panicked when she was questioned. Mind you, it still doesn't prove she did it.'

'No, but she's in it up to her neck with the inspector,' agreed Brent. 'Bang goes her alibi, no doubt about that. What do you think, Miss Gates?'

All thoughts of making Robert jealous vanished from her mind as she contemplated the latest problem facing the family.

'I think it would be best if we slept on it,' she decided at last, voicing their thoughts. 'I don't know about you, but I feel exhausted after all that.'

'Good idea,' approved Robert. 'Our minds might be a little clearer in the morning, after a good night's sleep. Try not to worry too much about it, Jill. Don't worry about me. Brent can drop me off on the way.'

Amid final farewells, Brent exclaimed admiringly, 'You certainly knew how to deal with those bouncers, Miss Gates. You were great.'

Smiling to herself, Jill opened the front door with her latch key, feeling happy that after all the unexpected events of the day, her encounter with Brent wasn't perhaps wasted after all.

7

IT DOESN'T MAKE SENSE

When he received Lark's report next morning, Inspector Platt was delighted.

'I knew it!' he greeted his superior, bursting with the news. 'I was right, after all.'

'What's all this?' enquired the chief constable good humouredly as he called in to hear the latest reports. 'Not like you to get excited so early in the day.'

Platt waved the tape recorder as if he was about to kiss it and placed it reverently on the desk in front of him. 'Listen to this, sir. It proves what I said. It was that Brenda Williams all the time.'

'Hm, seems to bear out what you said, sure enough,' agreed Mayfield, after listening to the recording. 'Who's that she's talking to? The voice sounds familiar.'

'Oh, that's that Bruce character I was telling you about and that handyman from the garage,' he said dismissively. 'Lark caught them at it in a session with that so-called friend of Brenda Williams – Daphne something or other. We've got it all down in black and white now. Care to join us, sir? I've got a warrant made out.'

'I wouldn't miss it for the world – I just hope you're right,' commented the chief constable. 'It's about time we had some results. Let's see what she has to say for herself. It sounds to me as if our young friend has solved the case for you.'

Unaware of the compliments being paid to him, Robert's mind was still full of conflicting arguments when he woke up. Although he was forced to accept the implications of Daphne's statement, he couldn't see Brenda going to such extreme lengths to get her own way. The more he thought about it, the more he was convinced that the case had the hallmarks of a man written all over it.

For a start, Brenda must have known Tom was left-handed. After all, they grew up together, and he couldn't imagine that she would have had the gumption to wipe her fingerprints off the gun afterwards. *It doesn't make sense*, he repeated to himself in exasperation. It had to be someone else, but who? What he needed right now was a shower to freshen himself up and to help him think straight, and a bite to eat before he could think of doing anything else. Then he would check with Brent to see if he had any new ideas, before seeing Jill.

In the event, Brent was out, probably at the garage he was told, so he set off to Rose Lodge. When he arrived, everyone was in a state of mild panic, expecting a visit from Inspector Platt any moment, with Brenda refusing to leave her room and no sign of Jill. Heaving a sigh, he begged a cup of coffee off Rose and settled himself in the study.

Within minutes, the front doorbell rang, and he heard Inspector Platt and two others being ushered into the drawing room. Almost immediately, Rose appeared looking flustered, asking him to join the visitors, while she went off in search of the Mistress.

Obeying the summons, Robert went in to discover the chief constable waiting patiently, seated in an armchair, while Platt was striding up and down, barking orders at Lark in passing.

'Ah, there you are.' Chief Constable Mayfield got up and greeted him with relief. 'I hear you've been up to your old tricks again, solving the case for us.' He waved Lark's tape recording at him cheerfully. 'According to this tape Lark made at that gambling den, that friend of Brenda's blew her alibi sky-high after you questioned her. Mind you, we won't go into the methods you used; it's the results that count.'

Listening to the recording, Robert made a mental note to get one himself, in case it came in handy at some point in the future.

His success was too much for his old adversary to bear and he immediately took it out on his subordinate. 'Lark, where's Mrs Williams?' he barked. 'Go and find her. Tell her it's important, I need to see her right away. I refuse to put up with her excuses any longer. And see if her husband is there. If he is, remind him I have a warrant …' He was about to repeat the phrase he had stored up in his mind ready for the occasion when he was interrupted by a scream and the sound of a falling body. 'Lark, what the devil?'

But his faithful hound was already at the door, peering out. 'Sir, I think you'd better come and see.'

They all rushed to the door, with Inspector Platt beating them by a short head. 'Out of my way, man. What the …?' In that split second, he realised bitterly that he would not have the pleasure of issuing his cherished summons after all for there, sprawling at the foot of the staircase, was all that was left of the late Brenda Williams.

At a sober gathering held afterwards while the doctor was examining the body, the chief constable broke the silence, saying drily, 'Looks as if that's crossed her off your chief list of suspects, eh Platt?'

The inspector shook his head stubbornly. 'With all due respect, sir, if I might be allowed to disagree, I still maintain she could be our culprit. Put yourself in her shoes. She was gambling heavily on the night in question. We have a recording from the witness, Daphne, stating she made threatening remarks about the deceased because he wouldn't buy that luxury holiday retreat she was on about, and she was up to her eyes in debt – what more do you want? My guess is that seeing the game was up, she decided to end it all and threw herself down the stairs. A case of suicide, pure and simple.'

'I grant you, there's a lot in what you say,' his superior said grudgingly. 'And it would account for a lot of things, but what was the motive?'

'Why, all that money of course, sir. She stood to earn a fortune.'

There was a discreet tap on the door and Doctor Meridew popped his head around the corner. 'I've finished my examination – all right to remove the body? I'll just write out my report.'

'Yes, go ahead, Doctor,' the Chief Constable agreed absently, still not completely satisfied in his mind.

As the stretcher party passed, it reminded Robert of something he'd noticed when they picked up her body and he had bent to take a closer look.

'That's odd,' he remarked thoughtfully, thinking back.

'What's that?' asked Mayfield keenly, his interest aroused.

'There was a funny looking mark on her ankle, as if ...' He broke off. 'If you'll excuse me,' he said and wandered out of the room.

'Well, that about wraps it up,' remarked the inspector, pleased with his version of events. 'I'll just get statements from the cook and anyone else who may have witnessed the incident.'

As he reached the top of the stairs, Robert bent down and picked up a strand of cord that attracted his attention. Peering closer, he saw that it was frayed at the edges where it had been stapled to the skirting board. He was still standing there, examining it pensively, when Rose approached and whispered in his ear, making him jump.

'It's Miss Jill.' She sounded anxious. 'I can't get her to answer and the bedroom door's locked.'

'Have you got a key?' he asked quickly, alarmed at her tone.

'No, but I can get one. I won't be half a jiff.'

He called after her, 'While you're at it, could you get the doctor to hang on? We might be needing him.' He waited impatiently, imagining all kinds of things that could have happened to her, when to his relief Rose came bustling up the stairs again with the doctor in her wake.

'Here we are, sir.' She inserted a key in the lock and opened the door nervously. 'Ah, there she is, sound asleep.' The relief in her voice was evident. She tiptoed over and gently shook Jill's shoulder. 'Wake up, Miss Jill. Gentleman to see you.'

Getting worried at the lack of response, she shook her again, just as the doctor entered the room.

'Let me see.' He took over, using his usual bluff assurance to diffuse the situation. He picked up a glass on the bedside table and sniffed at it. 'Looks to me as if she's had a knock-out drop of some kind. I'll check it out.' Noting their concern, he added cheerfully, 'Don't worry, I'll give you a shout when I've found out what's happened. Meanwhile, better let the inspector know.'

'Right,' promised Robert, 'we'll leave you to it. Come on, Rose.'

Re-entering the sitting room, he reported their discovery

and added grimly, 'Doc says he thinks Jill's been drugged. There was something in her glass.'

'What?' bristled the inspector, annoyed that his cherished verdict had been challenged, just as he'd thought he had the case nicely wound up.

'Excuse me, I think that's the doctor again,' decided Robert. 'I'd better see how she is.' As he left, he called over his shoulder absently, 'Oh, by the way, Inspector, that theory of yours is completely up the spout.' He dropped the tattered remains of the cord at their feet. 'That's what tripped her up – it wasn't suicide, she was *murdered*.'

After a pregnant pause, the chief constable picked it up thoughtfully. 'That's put the cat amongst the pigeons, wouldn't you say, Platt? Looks as if we'll have to start all over again if I'm not mistaken. You'd better get the fingerprint lads in to check the top of the stairs where that trap was set and don't forget the autopsy report; we'd better make sure of our facts. As if we haven't got enough on our plates.'

Just then, the front door opened, and Harold Williams appeared, clutching his briefcase. 'What *is* going on here? Haven't you finished yet with your infernal questioning? My wife will have something to say about this.'

The inspector turned to a fresh page in his notebook expectantly. 'Will you tell him or shall I, sir?'

Upstairs, Robert gathered Jill up in his arms. 'Thank heavens you're all right.' He looked up anxiously. 'She *is* okay now, Doctor?'

'Pulse and heartbeat back to normal, I'm glad to say. Mind you, my advice is to take it easy in the next few days, until the effects wear off.'

'Have you told her ...?'

The doctor nodded his head sombrely. 'Yes, just before you came. She was very lucky, if you ask me. It could have been far worse,' he mused aloud. 'My guess is that she might have got in someone's way, in view of what's been happening.'

Jill buried her head in Robert's shoulder and sobbed. 'And there I was being so beastly about her. What must you think of me? Oh, Robert, I feel awful,' she wept in a fresh outburst.

'Now then, take it easy, you weren't to know,' he consoled her. 'What can we do?' he appealed to the doctor.

'Don't worry, I'll give her a mild sedative to help her relax. Leave it to me.'

Robert gently disengaged her arms and stood up. 'If you would. I'd be very grateful.' I shan't be a minute,' he reassured her. 'I just want a quick word with the chief constable, and I'll be right back.'

'Promise?' she asked through her tears. 'I don't know what I'd do without you.'

He almost gave up at that point and nearly lost his head in an overwhelming urge to embrace her again and never let her go. 'Don't worry,' he said thickly. 'From now on, I'm not going to let you out of my sight. Just count the minutes, I won't be long.' He managed a smile and left the room quickly, afraid he might lose control if he stayed there any longer.

Downstairs, the inspector was discussing what to do next with the chief constable, after Brenda's husband had disappeared to the kitchen in search of a strong drink to drown his mixed emotions.

'You do realise, sir, they'll have to hold another inquest in view of the latest circumstances, which is bound to raise a number of questions about an unknown intruder, if that is the presumption, in light of the new facts.'

'I had already arrived at that conclusion,' replied the chief constable, irked at the long-winded phrases his subordinate used. 'It can't be helped. Meanwhile, I want you to organise a watch on this house right away, around the clock.'

The inspector showed his surprise. 'May I ask why, sir?'

'It's obvious, I would have thought. The murderer, whoever it is, is not likely to stop now. For all we know, he is probably looking for another victim.'

'With due respect, sir, I would suggest that we already have a likely suspect.'

'Oh, and who's that?'

'Why, the husband of course. He stands to inherit a small fortune now his wife is dead. Stands to reason.'

'I suppose there's something in what you say. You'd better question him as soon as he's got over the shock. But I have an uneasy feeling that's not the whole answer ...'

At that moment, Robert burst into the room, bringing them up to date with the latest position. 'You do realise, chief constable, that Jill's life is in danger. She's been drugged and needs our protection, now this murderer is on the loose again.'

'Don't worry, I've already seen to that. I've asked Platt to organise a strict watch on the house. He won't come near the place when he hears.'

Concerned at the state of Robert's appearance, he took him by the arm. 'Why don't you sit down and unwind and tell me about it? You look as if you could do with a drink.'

'No time for that, thanks all the same,' refused Robert, his mind elsewhere. 'I'll go and let Jill know – that should help to calm her down. On second thoughts, I think I'll ring my landlady and arrange to stay the night, if that's all right? I'd better let Rose know.' Having decided, he wheeled around and hurried back upstairs.

'Do you think that's wise, sir?'

'Wise, Platt, why ever not?'

'I have my reservations about that young man. I think I've

mentioned that before. I'm not sure that's a good idea, leaving him here overnight.'

'What utter rot. I don't see any problem with that. Why, if it wasn't for him and that young friend of his, we wouldn't have discovered that the alibi of Mrs Williams was a complete cover-up.'

'It didn't stop her from being murdered if I might point out, sir,' Platt persevered.

'And who discovered that, eh? You all assumed it was suicide.'

'That's as may be, sir. I'm still not happy about the present arrangements if you don't mind me mentioning.'

'If that's the case, you can always volunteer to stay the night yourself and keep an eye on him. Honestly, Platt, you're completely off the beaten track. Why, you can see the chemistry at work there with those two – nothing to do with crime. The boy's simply in love with her, can't you see that? You were young once.'

'In that case, I'll say goodnight, sir.' Stony-faced, the inspector left the room.

'At least, I suppose you were,' surmised the chief constable with a chuckle.

In his rush to get back, Robert bumped into Rose who stopped him with a warning glance.

'I shouldn't go in just now, sir. Doctor's given her something to make her sleep.'

'Oh, fair enough. Listen, Rose, I've decided to stay here tonight, if that's all right? Could you make a bed up for me? I'll go and collect some things and let my landlady know.'

'Right you are, sir. That'll please Miss Jill. She be awfully worried, not having a man about the place.' She brightened up.

'While you're at it, would you mind picking up a pie or something like that from the shops? We're getting a bit low in the larder, if you know what I mean, now we've got an extra mouth to feed, what with that there Sergeant coming along.'

'Of course, let me have a list, will you?'

Later, on his way back, he decided to call in and have a word with his uncle. *He must be wondering what's happening.*

He needn't have worried, his uncle was already abreast of the situation, living up to his reputation as an ex Det Sergeant.

'What a turn-up for the books,' he greeted his nephew. 'Poor old Brenda. Fancy her being a gambler all this time – she's the last person I would have expected. The number of times I've seen her hiding away his bottle of Scotch because she said it wasn't good for him. And that secretary of his having to put up with her sermons about not wasting a penny and making her do hand deliveries to save money on stamps, I ask you.' He mused aloud. 'Someone had it in for her – she couldn't have had many friends.'

'But I can't believe she would have gone to the lengths of shooting him. And she must have known he was left-handed. They grew up together; you wouldn't forget a thing like that.'

'No, that's true enough,' agreed his uncle. 'And where did she get the gun from? Tom wasn't into firearms. He didn't agree with them.'

'I can't help feeling that something's missing in this case,' declared Robert, puzzled. 'It doesn't add up. Why should it happen to one member of the family, being attacked after another? There has to be a reason.'

'Don't let's get involved in too many half-baked theories at this stage of the game,' advised his uncle. 'It's complicated enough as it is. So, old Harold cops the lot, eh? I suppose he's chief suspect, now our friend Platt's got nobody else to blame. Let's hope that young secretary of Tom is safe from it all. I don't know why she doesn't find herself another job, now she's got that little nest egg Tom left her.'

'She says she doesn't want to leave until she's cleared up the rest of Tom's affairs. The trouble is, while she stays, she may be putting herself in danger. She's already had a bit of a scare after someone slipped her that Mickey Finn. After that, we can't take any chances. We're making sure she has police protection. I've arranged to stay the night as we don't want anything else to happen to her,' he ended with determination, leaving no doubt about his feelings.

Uncle Ted cocked an eye knowingly. 'Oh, like that is it? When's the wedding? Keeping it a secret, are we?'

Robert flushed. 'I'm not in a position to offer her anything yet. If I managed to trace that missing daughter of Tom's, that might be the answer to everything, but it' a hell of a long shot.'

'That reminds me,' his uncle said with a furrowed brow. 'I never gave you the card from that enquiry agency. Did you ever get in touch?'

'No, it quite slipped my mind with all the recent drama,' Robert confessed. 'Thanks.' He slipped the card in his pocket and stood up. 'Is that the time? I've got to have a quick word with my landlady and pick up a few things. I'll pop over and let you know how I get on, as soon as it all quietens down a bit.'

After visiting the bank to get out some cash for the shopping, he remembered he never did call in to see that old lady on his list of people in need of help. Extracting a note from his wallet, he knocked on the door and glanced down at his shoes as he did so. *It's all very well helping others*, he admitted to himself, *when you can't even be bothered to put a bit of polish on your own shoes.* He was still scolding himself when the door opened, and a young face peered out fearfully.

'Ma's not in,' she said promptly and shut the door, but Robert had already anticipated such a move and wedged it open with his foot.

'Give her this when you see her.' He handed the note over kindly.

'Coo!' Her eyes widened with disbelief and, forgetting manners, allowed the door to swing back, giving him a glimpse of a figure lurking in the background. Advancing in a threatening manner, the woman shouted, 'I told you, "No hawkers", Sheila,' and made to slam the door.

Just as she was doing so, the child held up the note. 'See what the gentleman has just given me!'

The woman eyed him sternly. 'We're not selling anything, I told you. Be off with you.'

'It's nothing like that,' he said hastily. I'm from the "Help the Family". It was just a little something to put in the kitty.'

Her voice softened. 'That's different. Ever so good of you, sir. We don't get many of them, I'm sure.'

'Just for the record,' he said, his pen poised ready over his notebook. 'What name shall I say?' he added quickly at her look of suspicion. 'Just to ensure we know who's on our list, that's all.'

"Hickey, Bridget Hickey," she offered reluctantly. 'Now come along, Sheila, we've got work to do. Sister Kathleen will be here in half an hour. Thank the gentleman properly, mind.'

The little girl called Sheila just had time to give a half curtsy before the woman shut the door firmly in his face.

Robert thought no more of it but, later, as he was tucking in to a welcome supper provided by a devoted Rose, he recalled that Sheila was the name of the girl who cropped up in Tom's tale about his lost love.

It was a new and transformed Harold Williams who greeted him next day after getting back from the office, seemingly remarkably unaffected following the shock of his wife's unexpected death. Gone was his previous servile manner and in its place a more assertive version, as if he'd just begun to realise his new position.

'Ah there you are, Bruce, isn't it? Come in. I understand you're staying tonight, to look after us. Good man. Rose will see to your things. Rose,' he called out, 'Mr Bruce is here. Show him up to our guest bedroom and help him unpack.'

Barely lowering his voice, he announced grandly, 'I'm afraid we've got that sergeant of Platt's landed on us for the time being. Don't much approve of it myself – not good for my image, in my position.' He puffed out his chest. 'Things will be a bit different from now on, you'll see.' Warming to the prospect, he invited, 'When you're sorted out, come and have a glass or two and I'll explain my idea. Instead of that sergeant hanging around poking his nose into things that don't concern him, I've decided to have my own private army to look after things, now I can afford it. That'll put his nose out of joint. Get that young friend of yours to come and help guard the place. Looks a bit of a scruff to me, but I dare say I could make it worth his while. Give him a few bob extra than what they pay him at that dump of a garage where he works.'

Put off by this new side of Harold's character, compared with his previous obsequious manner, Robert made his way to the kitchen thoughtfully, vowing to have as little to do with the man as he possibly could as he meditated on the transformation of the once timid little husband. About to enter, he heard the unmistakable tones of Bates evidently agreeing with his feelings.

'I'm sorry, Miss Gates, I feel I must give in my notice. I can't stand the new master a moment longer and that's a fact.'

Her voice rose in protest. 'But Bates, you can't leave now, after all this time. There must be some sort of misunderstanding.'

'No, Miss, not after what he said to me just now. I said to

him, I says, I always prune the roses first thing, Master Williams I said, and he wouldn't listen to me. "You'll do as I says and like it" he told me, "or it's the door for you" he says. Just like that.'

'But, Bates, I'm sure he didn't mean it. Can't we sort something out? I don't know what we'd do without you.'

Making his presence known, Robert added his voice to her pleadings. 'You'd better stay, Bates. The place wouldn't be the same without you.'

Jill wheeled around gratefully. 'There you are! Mr Bruce agrees with me. Please overlook it, just this once. I'll speak to Mr Williams about it.'

Bates stood turning his hat over in his hands uncertainly. After a pause, he said gruffly, 'If you put it like that, Miss, I'll think it over like ... just this once, mind, just for you,' he added, and he shuffled out.

'I'm so glad you said that,' enthused Jill. 'Just look at the difference he's made since he's been here.'

She threw open the back door and sniffed appreciatively at the heady scent of the roses. 'Doesn't that show you what a goldmine he is?'

Robert took in the impeccable state of the lawn and the matching borders full of vibrant, attractive colours. 'Yes,' he agreed to keep her happy. 'I see what you mean.' Closing the door at last on the view and getting back to essentials, he eyed her searchingly. 'Now that we've got that settled, how do you feel?'

'Much better.' She stretched contentedly. 'That medicine the doctor gave me worked wonders. I feel so much better.'

'Good.' He nerved himself up to ask a question. 'If I get Brent to come over tomorrow and hold the fort, would it be all right if I checked up on that other matter Tom asked me to investigate? It all seems a bit quiet at the moment; otherwise I wouldn't ask.'

She traced a pattern on the bench where she had been

sitting and said rather coyly, 'Of course. He's rather a nice young man, when you get to know him. I expect we can find something to amuse ourselves with – unless, of course,' she added demurely, 'you want me to come with you.'

'No, that's quite all right,' he said, closing his eyes at the tantalising image. The thought of travelling anywhere with her within touching distance tormented him for a moment but, finally, he forced a smile. 'No, I'd rather you stay here where you'll be safe.'

She traced another pattern and looked up innocently. 'Wouldn't I be safe with you?'

'Of course,' he said hurriedly. 'It's just that I'll be rather busy ... checking things and seeing all sorts of people and asking questions and ...'

'Checking things?' She leant over and brushed his cheek with a light touch. 'Don't worry, I'll be a good girl. I'll look after him.'

8

A NEW WILL

Over a hasty breakfast, he quickly outlined the position to his friend Brent and explained what he wanted to do.

'Would I mind looking after that smashing bird of yours while you're out?' enthused the other. 'When do I start?'

Ignoring the implied suggestion, Robert glanced at his watch, calculating his next course of action. 'As soon as you like. If you drop me off at the station, I should be able to catch the 9:30. It's only three or four stops down the line, and then I can grab a taxi to,'—he read the card aloud—'"What's Your Problem" enquiry agency. What a weird name. I've already rung them, so they are expecting me. No need for you to come – just look after Jill and see she's safe."

'What are we waiting for then?' His friend rose, ready and eager.

Robert gazed at him sternly. 'You just watch it, mate. I'm relying on you, so don't let me down.'

Brent put up his hands in mock self-defence. 'Don't hit me! I'll guard her with my life.'

Relaxing, Robert gave him an affectionate punch. 'Come on then, off we go.'

~

An hour later, closeted with the manager of the enquiry agency, Robert explained his mission.

'Hm, twenty odd years ago, eh? That's going back a bit. Never mind. I got my girl to go through our files after you phoned and, hopefully, she may have come across what you're looking for.' He pressed a buzzer. 'Ah, Jenny, any luck? Right, let's have it. Bring it in.'

Turning over to the marked page, he exclaimed, 'Here we are, the "Tom Conway" enquiry.' He began, half reading to himself. 'I can see where the problem occurred. Our chap, who dealt with it, is retired long since, but he seems to have made a decent enough report. It says here that Conway became acquainted with a nurse called Sheila Hickey.'

Robert started and leant forward eagerly. 'Did you say "Hickey"? That's extraordinary, Tom didn't tell me that. Hickey is a most unusual name; what a remarkable coincidence. Did he find out where she lived?'

'Apparently, there were several in your area, one near where Conway was living at the time – in the High Street, according to his report. A highly respectable family, very straightlaced apparently. Yes, it happened when his wife ran off with someone called Willis. The result of their, um, liaison was a little girl born out of wedlock, so it says.'

'Yes, I know all about that. What happened to the girl?'

'Ah, that's where the problem arose. The family appeared to have ganged up on him and refused to grant him access or tell him anything about the child or her whereabouts. They were deeply religious, it seems. We had to give up in the end – it was like running into a brick wall. He must have spent a fortune over it.'

'I know,' sighed Robert, 'that's how he described it.'

'Have you tried this one it mentions in your village?'

'Only accidentally. I happened to call there in connection with a family charity I run.'

The manager closed the file apologetically. 'I'm sorry, we don't seem to have been much use.'

'Oh, you have,' disagreed Robert with a wry smile. 'It was there all the time, staring me in the face. Now all I have to do is to persuade them to give me the rest of the details.' He rose, shaking the other's hand. 'That's a different kettle of fish altogether.'

'I'm sorry we couldn't help you any further,' began the manager, putting the files together.

'Oh, but you can.' Robert was struck by a sudden thought. 'If we could find out anything more about this Sheila Hickey who lived there, that would give us a lead. All I know is that she was a nurse and the little girl who answered the door was called "Sheila" – there might be a family connection there. And,'—he consulted his notebook—'the woman with her gave her name as ... here we are, Bridget Hickey, if that's any help.'

The manager wrote the names down carefully. 'That's a start to go on. Leave it to me, Mr Bruce. Directly we come up with anything, I'll let you know. By the way, my name is Dan Bromley – here's my card. Meanwhile, don't hesitate to give me a call if I can help you in any way.'

On the way back, Robert decided to call in on his uncle to let him have the latest news, after remembering to go to the local electrical stores and investing in a miniature tape recorder he'd promised himself.

'Hm, pity they didn't give him that information when he consulted them in the first place,' was his uncle's verdict. 'Mind you, Tom always was a bit secretive about it at the time, probably wanted to protect the girl's reputation. Incidentally, we still haven't found out anything more about the murderer. I thought that was supposed to be our first priority? You'll never get anywhere as a private detective if you allow yourself to be lured off down any old blind alleyway. I should have a word with Reggie, if I were you, and see if he's come up with anything.'

Robert started guiltily. 'That reminds me, I forgot to tell you.' He entertained his uncle about the change that had taken place in Harold's attitude and about his offer.

'You'll be lucky if you get anything out of him,' was all his uncle would say. 'He's a right old scrooge. And make sure that friend of yours hasn't hijacked that girl of yours and taken her off to the pictures.'

'No, he promised to look after her,' Robert said, defending Brent.

'That's what I mean,' chuckled his uncle. 'I should grab her first, before *he* gets the chance.'

Directly he got back however, he was met with a bombshell that drove any other idea he may have had out of his head.

'You'll never guess what we've found.' Jill was nearly beside herself with excitement. 'We've discovered a new will! I was looking for stamps in the study and there it was, stuck in the back of a drawer.' She waved it around her head as proof.

'Careful,' warned Robert cautiously, 'you might damage it. We'd better contact our solicitor. Let me see ... is it properly witnessed?'

Jill perused the document. 'Yes, it says here, witnessed by Rose Bennet. Why that's the cook ... and who is that?' She peered more closely at the signature. 'Looks like James Bites – no Bates, our gardener. Why didn't we know about this?'

Robert was puzzled. 'Yes, that sounds odd. I'd better ring

Arbuthnot. Funny, he didn't know about it. I wonder if he's there. I'll find out – I've got his number somewhere.'

After trying unsuccessfully several time he finally got through. 'Damn, he's with a client at the moment. His secretary says he'll ring back. While I'm waiting, I'd better ring Platt. No,' his face clouded over. 'He'll only make some daft remark and say it's all my fault – I think this calls for the chief constable.'

'You will?' he repeated after making contact. Covering the phone with his hand, he announced with great satisfaction, 'He'll call in on his way home.'

Just as he put it down, it rang again. 'Is he free now? Hello, is that you, Henry? Good. Listen, you'll never guess. Jill's just found a new will. Yes, two witnesses. You will? No, I meant, you'll come?'

He swung around. 'They're on their way. Golly, that's a full house. No, you'd better let me keep it for the moment. I can't understand the small print; we'd better wait and let Henry tell us what it means.'

'Gosh, d'you think he changed his mind?' Jill flung her arms out wide, posing dramatically. 'I know, he's left it all to a cat's home and we don't get anything, after all.'

'I doubt it.' Robert was more practical. 'It's probably something he's forgotten to include in the first one – we'll soon know. Ah, that sounds like one of them,' he added as a car was heard to pull up outside.

But it turned out to be someone much closer to home. A few minutes later, the latch clicked, and the front door flew open, revealing a highly indignant Harold, brandishing his briefcase. 'What the devil is going on here the moment my back is turned? I've only got to be out of the house for five minutes before something happens. What, may I ask, is the chief constable doing, coming back here again? And that blasted solicitor as well. Haven't they got a home to go to? As if we haven't seen enough of them. I was hoping to get some peace and quiet after a hard day at the office, and what do I get?'

Robert stepped forward diplomatically to break the news. 'Jill has just found a new will.'

'What?' Harold's face betrayed his fears. 'I still get the money, don't I – I mean w-what does it say?'

'We're waiting for the solicitor to tell us.'

Harold flung off his overcoat. 'Well, don't just stand there; we'd better get inside and hear what he has to say, if we can understand the usual jargon. Tell Rose we don't want any interruptions on any account.'

After a lengthy perusal of the document, Henry Arbuthnot commented, 'As I should have guessed, it's a necessary footnote to make sure he hadn't forgotten anything, in the event of certain unexpected contingences arising.'

'What would those be in plain English?' demanded Harold tensely, before anyone could speak.

The solicitor adjusted his spectacles. 'Let me see. For instance, should the remaining beneficiary pass away – in this case, yourself,'—he inclined his head towards Harold—'and providing you had no issue, the inheritance would pass to his former wife, Sylvia.'

'What?' squawked Harold, outraged. 'Not to that wretched Sylvia! We'll see about that.' His voice could hardly be heard above the ensuing gasps that broke out.

'B-but, they were divorced!' Robert found himself objecting in his astonishment.

'Not according to this,' commented the solicitor drily. 'I was going to bring up the matter at the next meeting, but we had to put it back because of subsequent, um, developments. The truth of the matter is, that because of the break-up and the unfortunate death of Conway's intended, the whole matter seems to have been left in abeyance over the years and nothing was done about it. Highly irregular, I might add.' His lips pursed in disapproval. 'On top of that, according to his bank, he has been paying all his former wife's bills while she has been looked after in hospital over the past couple of years.'

'So, what you are saying,' added Robert slowly, 'is that Sylvia or her family are legally entitled to Tom's inheritance if …' He glanced at Harold meaningly.

'Exactly,' agreed the solicitor. 'Although, as far as we are aware, the lady has no family of her own. The man she eloped with,'—he glanced at his notes—'a "Richard Willis", died some years ago from pneumonia. And the only surviving relative, his offspring, died in a skiing accident.'

'So that appears to rule them out,' said Robert, summing up. 'That'll give something else for the inspector to worry about.'

'You are forgetting that other little matter that came up at the meeting,' reminded Henry Arbuthnot, turning over to the next page.

'Of course, you mean the missing girl.'

'Precisely.' He turned to explain to the others. 'At the last meeting, I informed you all about a sum of £30,000 to be held on trust for the benefit of Mr Bruce, should he be successful in his quest to discover the whereabouts of the missing daughter that Mr Conway was anxious to locate. What we did not have time to announce was that a trust fund has also been set aside for the benefit of the missing daughter, whoever she might be, once her identity has been established beyond doubt. My client never gave up hope on finding her and over the years it has grown to a significant amount, as you might imagine. Of course,' he added, 'I shall have to question the two people who witnessed the will to ensure that this version is a genuine one and carried out quite legally.'

'Quite right,' echoed the pompous tones of Harold Williams, emerging from his blissful daydream. 'Let's have a word with that cook of ours for a start.'

'Let me do that,' offered Jill eagerly. 'And I'll get hold of Bates at the same time.'

She disappeared in her mission, just as the front doorbell rang.

'That'll be the chief constable,' guessed Robert. 'I'll let him in.'

'That sounds a most remarkable development,' commented Mayfield when Robert came to the end of his tale. 'I wonder what Platt will make of that. I'd better get him over here and see what he has to say.'

He'll go spare was Robert's immediate reaction, but he kept the thought to himself.

The door opened and Rose entered nervously, bobbing her head respectfully, looking apprehensively at the row of faces ranged in front of her.

'Yes, sir?' she directed her appeal, hopefully, at the homely figure in charge.

'We just want to ask you a few questions,' stated the chief constable kindly, doing his best to put her at her ease.

'Yes, sir.'

'Did you at any time get asked by your late Master to sign any type of document?'

She shook her head anxiously. 'No, sir, only a receipt for some of the tradesmen, like. Everything as it should be. He was the best Master I've ever had.'

'Quite so. What I'm asking about has nothing to do with the tradesmen, as you put it. I was thinking more on the lines of a legal document.'

'I don't know about that, sir. He never bothered me about such matters. Mr Arbuthnot is the gentleman you should be talking to,' she added, clearly wanting to help out.

'Yes, I'm aware of that,' he said patiently. 'The type of document I'm talking about would be something like this.' He held up the copy of the will they had been discussing.

'Oh, that, sir.' Her eyes lit up in recognition. 'I seem to recollect I see'd one of them before. Now where was it – it'll come to me in a minute.'

'When was that? Take your time and tell us all about it.'

'It was about that time when someone went and done in the Master. It gives me nightmares just to think about it, horrible it was.'

'Yes ...?' he prompted. 'What do you remember in particular? Something to do with a will, was it?'

'It never crossed my mind until you showed it to me.'

'Just tell us in your own words, Rose. Did your Master want you to witness something?'

She shook her head vigorously. 'No, nothing like that, sir. It was in the morning, just after breakfast.' She paused in an effort to remember. 'I was just clearing up to get ready to go out – it was my afternoon off that day, if you see what I mean.'

'Yes, go on.'

'I always want to make sure everything is shipshape afore I leave, when the Master stops me and asks me if I've got a moment to spare. I always had a moment for that man, whatever it was. And he asks me if I could sign a bit of paper, like. I couldn't make head or tail of it and I was just going to sign it where he directed me, when he said "hold on, we need another signature", and just at that moment, blow me if Bates didn't stroll by putting his rake away. Said he had to clear up proper like 'cause he was going to ask the Master if he could have some time off to go and see his cousin who was down with flu, so he told me.'

'Yes, then what?' asked the chief constable, his patience beginning to run out.

'Yes, well, he sat me down in his study and got me and Bates to sign at the bottom where there were a cross. So, we did.' She looked up triumphantly, pleased to get it off her chest at last.

'Did you notice what the paper was all about?'

'No, sir. I was looking at the clock all the time, afraid I was going to miss me coach outing. Bates will tell you, won't you, James,' she said, catching sight of him entering the room.

'Thank you, Rose, that was splendid. I'll get Platt to take down your statement for you to sign when he arrives. Nothing to worry about; we just need to get it on record.'

'Thank you, sir. May I go now?'

'Yes, of course. I think we could all do with a cup of tea now, don't you?'

'Yes, sir. I'll see to that right away,' she agreed hastily, keen to get away to her kitchen and the reassuring sounds of the kettle and all the other comforting background noises.

'I imagine you heard all that and know what I want, eh Bates?' the chief constable asked.

'Yes, sir. You want me to sign a statement like what Rose agreed to when the inspector arrives.'

'Exactly. Did you manage to see what the paper was all about, by the way?'

'No, sir. T'weren't none of my business. I was wanting to get away to see my cousin. She was down with the flu and taken bad, so they said.'

'So I understand. I trust she is better now?'

'Yes sir, I was able to get away to go to Master's funeral. I wouldn't have missed that for the world.'

'That will be all then, Bates. All I need now is a statement from you both for the records.'

'Yes, sir, thank you, sir. Can I go now and finish me digging? I'm keen to get the spuds in before I'm off.'

'Off you go then.'

As the door closed behind him, Rose came in and set the tray down. 'Would you like me to pour now, or shall I leave it?'

'No, I could do with one now, after all that. Oh, and you'd better get another cup, Rose. That sounds like the inspector.'

'Yes, well if you'll excuse me, gentlemen.' Harold heaved

himself to his feet ponderously. 'I think I'll have a bath and get rid of the London grime. It'll give me a chance to freshen up and think over what this new will really means.' He snorted. 'The infernal cheek, "leave it to Sylvia" indeed. I thought wills were supposed to be simple jobs – no need for solicitors and their mumble jumble, wasting our time.'

'Of course, Mr Williams, you go and freshen up. Tea, Arbuthnot?'

'The solicitor looked at his watch and apologised. 'No, if you don't mind, I'd better get back to the office and deal with the "mumble jumble", as our friend calls it.' He exaggerated the phrase humorously. 'I'll take the will with me, if I may? If you need anything explaining, give me a bell.'

'Ah Platt, we were just talking about you,' he greeted as the inspector strode in, looking distinctly ruffled. 'Apparently, there's been a new development. Another will has come to light, thanks to Miss Gate here. Take a look at that. Oh, sorry, I'd forgotten that Arbuthnot had to take it with him for safe keeping. Briefly, this is what it's all about.' He went over details of the new will and concluded grimly, 'It looks as if we have one or two new motives that we didn't know about.'

'As you say, sir.' The inspector glanced meaningly at the others. 'In the light of what you say, sir, I would suggest that we go into it more thoroughly back at HQ, after I've taken down those statements. If you'll excuse me.'

'Perhaps you're right, Platt. It will give us more time to check on the facts.' He bowed to Jill. 'All thanks to you, Miss Gates, for uncovering this valuable new piece of evidence.' Nodding at Robert, he added, 'Let me know if you have any new information that might prove useful.'

'Will do, sir.'

Once the efficient inspector had re-appeared with the necessary statements and departed, Robert watched the tail-lights of the car disappear.

'Now, before Harold makes an appearance, why don't we see what Rose has got lined up for us in the kitchen? I don't know about you, but I feel a bit peckish. I've had enough excitement to last me for a week.'

'What a good idea,' Jill exclaimed feelingly. 'Now that Harold and Platt are out of the way, I think we'd better make the most of it. A little breathing space is just what we all need, don't you think, Brent?' she said to Brent, who had been sitting quietly while all this was happening.

'You're absolutely right, Miss Gates,' he agreed, helping her up, watched by his friend with a pang of envy.

To take his mind off the spectacle, Robert decided to have a word with Rose to see what she had to offer.

'I've got a nice steak and kidney pie left over, just enough for the three of you, sir,' she reported with a beaming smile.

'What about you, Rose?' He felt guilty.

'Don't you worry about me, sir,' she was quick to reassure him. 'I've already had mine. I wasn't expecting anyone else to drop in.'

As if endorsing her remark, there was a crash outside and the door burst open, catapulting two young figures into the room and ending up sprawling at their feet.

'Bates caught 'em red-handed, climbing over the fence,' announced Sergeant Lark, poking one of them with his truncheon.

'And I recognised this 'ere,' echoed Bates, jabbing the other with his rake. 'It's one of them young villains from the garage, mate of that one,' he accused, nodding at Brent. 'I told you it was him, didn't I?'

The latter sprang to his feet, annoyed at being interrupted in his cosy chat. 'Phil, what are you doing here?'

'Came along with Gus here, didn't I?' was the aggrieved response. 'Didn't want to miss anything, after all that talk down in the pub.'

'Can you identify either of these intruders, sir?' Sergeant Lark asked Robert, getting out his notebook as Gus struggled to his feet.

'No, but I can,' apologised Brent. 'I can vouch for Phil. He works down at the garage with me.'

'Pity he don't knock at the front door, like anyone else,' commented the sergeant darkly, seeing his hopes of promotion dashed. Doing his best to retrieve the situation, he rallied and asked formally, 'Then can I ask you to bring him down to the station, sir, to answer one or two questions?'

'Of course.'

'And this young man?' he asked, nodding at Gus.

Relieved that he was about to get Jill to himself again, Robert was quick to tell a few white lies in defence of his friend. 'I expect he'd heard that I'd been trying to get in touch with him. We both work for Home Stores, or I did until recently.'

'Oh, that's all right then, young man. You're free to go in that case,' said the sergeant, addressing his remarks to Gus, who was deciding whether to take a chance and make a run for it.

'Thanks for that.' He wiped his forehead in relief as he watched the others march off. 'I thought I'd had it for a moment.'

'What did you do a silly thing like that for?' demanded Robert after they'd gone. 'I was thinking of getting in touch with you to give me a hand with something that's cropped up, but I thought you'd be too busy with all your overtime.' He nearly added 'and girlfriends' but thought better of it.

'Too busy? I like that,' snorted his friend. 'When they stopped that delivery of ours to Rose Lodge, I got the push, didn't I?'

'Sorry, I didn't know, but now you're here ...' He thought over Bates's warning about Brent and came to a sudden decision. 'I think I might have something for you to do after all. Keep in touch and I'll give you a ring.'

Having settled that little problem, he turned in anticipation of a cosy meal alone with Jill, when in stumped the last person he wanted to see.

Rubbing his hands at the sight of Rose bearing down on them with a tray loaded with dishes giving off an appetising smell, Harold broke the spell with a hearty, 'Splendid, my favourite. That was well timed – how did you know I was coming?'

Robert groaned at the sight.

9

LIVEN THINGS UP

At Police Headquarters, Inspector Platt was experiencing a similar mood of frustration. 'Lark? Any more developments in the Rose Lodge case?'

'Only the report of those young villains breaking in unlawfully, sir. I've questioned that Brent lad and his friend Phil, but it all seems pretty harmless – more of a lark, I would say. Nothing much happening in the village at the moment, apparently. He says he was looking for something to liven things up.'

'That's what we could do with around here,' commented the chief constable, overhearing the last remark as he entered. 'Who's that you're talking about?'

'Good afternoon, sir,' said Inspector Platt, springing to attention. 'Just a minor break-in by a couple of locals. Nothing we need worry about.'

'Let me see, I'll be a judge of that. Hm-mm.' The chief constable sat back thoughtfully, reading it through. 'A lad from the garage eh? Isn't that where that Brent fellow works – a friend of Robert? I see the gardener doesn't think much of him. Is it true what they're saying in the village about him?'

'I haven't heard anything about that, sir,' said Inspector

Platt, catching his drift. Seeing an opportunity to have a dig at Robert, he added pointedly, 'but if you remember, sir, he was the one who provided an alibi for Robert Bruce about repairing his heating system at the time Conway was murdered.'

'And he was the one who drove Mrs Williams to that gambling den,' recalled the chief constable, 'where she claimed to have an alibi for the same event.'

'Yes sir,' exclaimed Platt, warming to the theory. 'That also leaves us with a security problem I was going to tell you about. If you remember, Mr Williams has asked him to stay on at Rose Lodge tonight to give him extra protection.'

'So he has, by Jove. That needs thinking about. Incidentally, this report of Lark's is first-rate. I'm surprised you haven't promoted him to Det Sergeant by now.'

'He may be all right on paperwork, but he hasn't got it up here, where it counts,' said Platt dismissively, tapping his head. 'We could all do with a bit of promotion, if you go by that,' he added feelingly, thinking it was about time he dropped a hint or two on the subject.

Mayfield snorted. 'We don't seem to have got very far with solving this case, if that's what you mean,' he said, leaving Platt feeling more frustrated than ever.

'With respect, I must disagree with you there,' carried on Platt hopefully. 'We had plenty of suspects to start with, but just as we were about to make an arrest, the suspect let us down.'

'How unfortunate,' commented the chief constable sarcastically. 'Have we anyone left?'

Taking his remark seriously, Platt pointed out patiently, 'As I mentioned before, sir, the most likely suspect is still Mr Williams. He's the one who stands to gain most so far. If you remember, he still hasn't provided an alibi for the time he left the gambling den on the night in question.'

'Nor did his wife, and look what happened to her.'

Undaunted by his superior's comments, the inspector

ploughed on. 'Also, he inherits a sizeable amount from the death of his wife if you remember. And if we are to believe this latest will that's just been discovered, he could stand to inherit a small fortune, even if Bruce fails to locate that daughter of Conway.'

'Which, in turn, makes him a prime target, if we are still looking for someone else to fit the description of the murderer's next victim,' interrupted his superior.

'As you say, he could be the next one on the list,' agreed the inspector. 'But who else is there?'

'True,' Mayfield reflected. 'What about this Brent chap? Do you think he poses a danger?'

'We haven't got anything on him in our records to suggest otherwise,' Platt admitted. 'But if I might make a suggestion?'

'Go on.'

'I believe Williams possesses a small dressing room adjacent to his bedroom. With your permission, I suggest we get Lark to sleep there tonight and be on his guard, ready to deal with any intruders, sir.'

The chief constable sighed. 'Go ahead, if you think Williams will put up with it. You heard what he said about not wanting the police about the place.'

'He will if he knows his life depends on it,' said Platt importantly. 'Leave it to me.'

When it came down to it, the prospect of having the sergeant prowling around in the middle of the night on the lookout for intruders did not appeal to anyone when it was first announced, least of all, Harold. As everyone expected, he exploded in a furious fit of rage and, initially, would have nothing to do with it. It took the personal appearance of the inspector himself to point out the alternative consequences, plus a heavily sedated drink from Rose, before he would allow himself to be led away, grumbling, to bed.

As Jill pointed out in a fit of giggles before they followed his example, 'I hope the sergeant takes his boots off before he starts prowling.'

The trouble with the sergeant, however, was that he was too conscientious. He was acutely aware that he needed to distinguish himself if he was to achieve that much sought-after promotion he'd set his heart on, and he saw this as his opportunity. Not content with tiptoeing around at regular intervals to satisfy himself that all was well, he decided to equip himself with a flashlight and started thrusting it under Harold's nose in bed, turning it on at regular intervals to make sure, just as his long-suffering victim was vainly trying to get off to sleep. After his third round of inspection, he was just getting into the swing of things when Harold decided enough was enough.

Throwing his bedclothes aside, he grabbed the flashlight and started battering the sergeant's head with it in a frenzied attack. The next minute, he found himself in handcuffs and was led off protesting to finish the night in the local police cell.

'Well,' said Robert ruefully, surveying the piled-up bedclothes and the empty bed after sounds of the departing police car faded away, 'I can't see us getting to sleep after that.'

Peering over his shoulder Jill agreed, yawning. She glanced at her watch. 'Why don't I make us a drink while we decide what to do?'

'Sounds a good idea,' supported Brent, appearing sleepily from the other room. 'Why don't we all have one? I'll get a tray.'

Sitting cosily in the kitchen, borrowing some bedclothes to keep warm, they sat sipping their drinks and looking at each other, half awake.

'Well,' asked Jill at last, 'we've still got half the night in front of us; how are we going to pass the time?'

'We could play cards,' suggested Brent half-heartedly after a pause. 'Anyone interested?'

Jill giggled, sharing a secret. 'We did that last Christmas and found we had so many packs mixed up that Brenda threw a fit and had the whole lot thrown away.'

They looked at each other, seeking inspiration.

Then an idea struck Robert. He knew nothing about Jill or where she came from – she'd always been vague about it when they had touched on the subject before. This seemed like a good opportunity to find out. Trying not to sound too obvious, he said, 'Why don't we take it in turns to tell each other something about ourselves – you know, where we come from and all that background stuff. It'll help to pass the time and might be interesting, you never know.' Seeing them hesitate, he plunged on, 'I'll start.'

At his words, the other two relaxed and sipped their drinks expectantly.

'You know me.' He paused, wondering where to begin. 'I'm Robert Bruce – nothing to do with that well-known Scottish King from way back,' he added with a laugh. 'I'm twenty-two next month and I'm the last one in my family, apart from Uncle Edward who, as you all know, was a Det Sergeant before he retired. My mother, Margaret, bless her heart, had cancer and I lost her five years ago. Then my dad, who was a partner in a firm of solicitors – all with the help of dear old Tom – passed away two years ago. All rather sad and depressing. I miss them both dreadfully, but that's life. Have I missed anything?'

'You didn't tell us anything about your other less publicised activities, like giving handouts to people down on their luck and looking for a helping hand,' reminded Jill.

'Oh that,' dismissed Robert, embarrassed. 'We all go through that at some point in our lives. It's just my way of paying some of it back.'

'I know what you mean,' replied Jill pensively. 'I was in the same position at one time – if it hadn't been for Tom, bless him, I don't know what I would have done.'

'Is that something you could tell us about?' asked Robert gently. 'Or does it bring back painful memories – don't tell us if you'd rather not.'

'It's not that,' she reflected. 'It all seems lost in the mists of time. Since I've been with Tom, he was like a whole family rolled up in one. Anything before that is so unreal. All I remember is a brief flash I get sometimes, when I was a baby and there was someone bending over me. She had such a kind face, but at times rather severe, if you know what I mean.'

'Did she have a name?' asked Robert tentatively. 'Like Mary or Rose, or something like that, or was she a nurse?'

Jill tried to concentrate and had to give up apologetically. 'I thought I heard the name "Sheila" mentioned in the background on one occasion, but I couldn't be sure.'

Robert felt a tingle of excitement at the news but was cut short by a burst of recognition by Brent. 'I remember that too, but I can't remember any names.' He broke off. 'Sorry, it brought it all back to me when I was in that orphanage.'

To Robert's disappointment, the attention switched to his friend while he was still trying to grapple with the fleeting mention of Sheila and what it could mean. If true, it opened up an entirely new concept of what he knew about Jill. But then he remembered what Tom had told him about Sheila's family packing the girl off to an orphanage in Ireland and his theory came tumbling down like a pack of cards. Could it be true? If so, surely she would have had an Irish accent? Listening to her now, there was no trace of it. He shook his head; it looked as if he must wash that one out.

Suddenly aware of two pairs of eyes fixed on him, expecting him to comment, he made haste to cover up. 'What was the name of the orphanage ... er, Brent,' he found himself babbling.

To his relief, he saw his question had taken the other by surprise.

'Funny you should ask that,' debated Brent, treating the question seriously. 'That was the same thing I asked when I found out. But they refused to tell me. I was told my mother, whoever she was, wanted to keep it a secret for some reason. I was adopted, but it's never the same thing. I would have loved to have known.'

'So would I,' confessed Jill, sharing his disappointment.

Realising they were not likely to get any further, and in view of the emotional distress it was causing, Robert decided to wind the discussion up.

'I don't know about you two, but I'm feeling a bit washed up. Why don't we grab a few hours' sleep, what's left of it, before they decide whether to let Harold go?'

'Yes,' Jill decided with a firm nod, standing up. 'I don't want him to find us like this when he gets back – he'll blame it all on us, knowing him.'

Brent was quick to agree. 'I could do with a kip. Don't forget we've got that inquest of Brenda's on Saturday.'

Amid groans as they made their way up the stairs, Robert reminded them, 'Depends whether they want Harold to attend or not. He is next of kin, don't forget.'

In the event, it was decided not to issue Harold with a summons to attend after all; as it turned out, he had an alibi for the time Brenda met her death. Two witnesses presented themselves at the police station the next day, ready to attest to the fact that they fell into conversation with Harold as he got off the train on the day in question and chatted with him up to the time he entered his front door.

This information greatly relieved the inspector, who feared

Harold might have started complaining about his sergeant waking him up with a flashlight every time he tried to get to sleep, ending up with him spending the night in police custody.

Beginning to get quite used to the idea of facing up to the penetrating gaze of the coroner, namely Alastair Bunning, the local magistrate, Robert was quite miffed to discover that the inspector was prepared to take full credit for discovering how Brenda met her death by setting off a tripwire, instead of committing suicide as he had originally claimed. But after keen questioning by the magistrate, the inspector was forced to admit the true facts and Robert once more found himself in the witness box.

'Now, Mr Bruce, I understand from the inspector that you were the first to discover the true nature of the death of the deceased?'

'Yes, I believe that is true,' he replied, carefully ignoring the look of baffled fury on the inspector's face as he sat in the audience, despite his studied air of indifference.

The magistrate held up his hand to still the buzz of voices. 'If certain members of the audience will bear with us, perhaps you would tell us in your own words how you arrived at this conclusion.'

'It was when the stretcher party passed the open door of the drawing room where we were sitting,' he began. 'I remembered I'd seen a red mark and an unusual swelling on one of the deceased's ankles when we found her. It seemed a little odd, so I went upstairs to have a decko.'

'By that remark, I take it you decided to investigate,' corrected the learned magistrate, to an outbreak of titters from the front row.

'Exactly,' agreed Robert, keeping a straight face. 'When I got to the top landing, I found the remains of what appeared to be a trip cord still attached to the woodwork by the top step. I passed the evidence over to the inspector to examine, pointing out that the initial diagnosis needed to be reassessed.'

Although he put it as politely as he could without causing further embarrassment to the inspector, he could tell that it was not well received, judging by the sudden twitching of limbs emanating from the gentleman in question.

'Thank you for your most lucid explanation of the tragedy, Mr Bruce. I have no doubt that your assessment as to the cause of death will have been welcomed by the police and will receive due recognition. You may step down, thank you. Now can we hear the result of the autopsy? Doctor Meridew, I believe.'

When the day of Brenda's funeral followed, people were speculating about the absence of Harold.

Some of the villagers were spreading the rumour that he was in police custody still, while others were of the opinion that he had done a bunk – some were even convinced he had been spotted living it up in some South American gambling den. But as the service began, there he was in person, paying tribute to his dearly beloved wife, as he put it, with only a few scratch marks on his wrists to show where the handcuffs had been. He even managed a brave smile, acknowledging the good wishes of the departing mourners as they filed past him after the service.

But when the time for the reading of Brenda's will came a few days later, he was back to his normal overbearing presence, finding excuses to contradict or condemn anything the solicitor had just announced.

"Speak up" or "that's nonsense" were the terms he invariably used when he couldn't think of anything else to say. And when he caught sight of Sergeant Lark diligently patrolling the aisles as instructed by the inspector, he would bark, 'Show that man out – who let him in?'

It got to the point where Henry Arbuthnot, the ever-patient solicitor, felt like tearing his hair out, as he confided to Robert after the hearing. 'Good luck to him is all I can say, now he's got his hands on his wife's inheritance,' he pronounced wearily. 'Whatever's left of it, after all their gambling habits.'

'He's got nobody to leave it to, has he,' said Robert sadly, thinking what his old friend Tom would have said about it. 'He'll probably blow the lot, knowing him.'

'I'm afraid I must disagree with you on that point,' countered the solicitor without thinking.

''What are you talking about, Henry – you know Brenda couldn't stand having children about. Who else would he leave it to?'

Realising what he had just said, the solicitor added quickly, 'Forget what I said; that was in strict confidence.'

'But Henry, you can't get away with that.' Robert was bewildered. 'Everyone knew she wouldn't have any children. She made that perfectly clear to Harold, although I always suspected he would have hankered after a son of his own. But you're quite right – he wouldn't have dared go against Brenda's wishes.'

'He must have changed his mind then,' speculated his friend, 'after what he's just told me.'

Despite Robert's entreaties, he refused to say anything more on the subject. It wasn't until the following week that he found out why.

After a few days, everything seemed to get back to normal. Harold departed for the office every day, as was his custom, and came back suitably exhausted after a hard day, as he described it, to be remedied by a relaxing bath, followed by a strong drink and a liberal helping of his favourite dish, steak and kidney pie. Even the inspector gave up insisting on his sergeant staying the night as an added precaution.

It was not until the following Monday, when that routine was interrupted. Gone was the expected sound of his key in the latch, denoting his return, and by eight o'clock even Rose was concerned that his steak and kidney pie had gone cold, despite repeated warm-ups.

Feeling alarmed at his absence, Robert reported his misgivings to the police, and then to the inspector, and within half an hour the news was relayed back that Harold had met with an accident.

Tired of all the snippets of news that continued to filter through on the phone, Robert advised Jill and Brent to call it a day and wait to see what the morning would have to offer.

It was a harassed and bitter inspector who called in after breakfast to bring them the latest news. 'If only he'd listened to me,' he kept repeating. 'I warned him, didn't I? You'll all bear witness to that – even when I went to the trouble of arranging Lark to guard him overnight,' he added, conveniently forgetting the havoc it had caused.

'Yes, but you haven't told us yet what's happened,' reminded Robert, beginning to think they would never find out from the inspector, given his present state.

'I'm telling you; he was standing on his usual platform at London Bridge, waiting for the train to come in, when ... ugh.'

'What happened?' urged Jill with a sudden premonition, holding onto Robert for support.

'Why don't you go and get Rose to bring us a cup of tea?' he suggested soothingly, pointing her in the direction of the kitchen.

'No, I must hear,' she insisted. 'Go on, Inspector.'

'It happened so quickly, it was difficult for anyone to be

sure, but there was some sort of scuffle and the next minute, so I have been informed, he stumbled or was ... um ... pushed in front of the next train coming in.'

'So, we don't know whether it was an accident or deliberate,' concluded Robert, doing his best to shield Jill.

'No,' was the reluctant admission. 'There was a constable on duty at the station at the time, as it happened, but he couldn't lay his hands on anyone who would be prepared to make a statement.'

He banged his stick on the table in his frustration. 'Mark my words, it'll turn out to be one of those cases where it ends up as an accident, blast it, and nobody will ever know.'

And it appeared as if his forecast was correct.

As he reviewed the latest results at his next meeting with the chief constable, he predicted moodily, 'I expect the only one who'll be satisfied the way things are turning out is the wretched murderer himself, if there is one, now the last member of the family has been polished off. So, what I'd like to know,' he asked resignedly, 'is where do we go from here?'

'You may be right,' agreed the chief constable, 'but I've got a funny feeling we haven't seen the last of this legacy business.'

In the event, he was proved right, for the biggest bombshell of all came at the reading of the will, following a subdued funeral where they all put in an appearance, despite Harold's unpopular standing in the village.

'Why are we going?' objected Jill when it was proposed.

'Because of something the solicitor said to me the other day,' said Robert firmly. 'He rang me this morning to make sure we'd be there. We'd better turn up; otherwise we might miss something.'

'Oh, all right, if you insist.' Jill relented. 'But I still don't understand why. You've never liked the man.'

'That's true,' admitted Robert, 'but I've got a funny feeling that we're going to learn something to somebody's advantage, as the saying goes.'

If Henry Arbuthnot noticed them joining the small gathering, he made no sign of it. Instead, he proceeded to read out the contents of the will that was to shatter all their preconceived ideas.

After going through the preliminaries, he broke off and smiled at them disarmingly. 'Having got that off my chest, I will explain why he made certain alterations to his will only quite recently.' He glanced around the room as if making sure that there were no unfamiliar faces present to hear the personal details of what was to follow. 'If you remember, Miss Gates—who I am glad to see is with us today—was clever enough to discover the existence of another will by my old friend, the late Tom Conway. In it, he directed that if the last member of his family were to pass on, that the residue of his estate would be bequeathed to his nearest relative, assumed to be his former wife Sylvia, whom he never actually divorced. When my late client Harold Williams learned about this, he was so incensed he instructed me to contact his surviving dependants and make them his beneficiaries.'

This was too much for Jill to accept. 'But Harold didn't have any dependants. Brenda made sure of that.'

'Ah, but I fear I must correct you there. According to Mr Williams, his late wife gave birth to twin boys in the early days of their marriage.'

'Are you sure – he wasn't having you on?' exclaimed Robert in disbelief.

'Oh yes, quite sure. I have a written statement from my client to that effect.'

'Goodness, what happened to them,' joined in Jill, equally astounded.

'I'm coming to that.' He consulted his papers. 'It seems that his wife refused to accept the situation and insisted the twins should be adopted to relieve them of any further responsibility.'

'But didn't Harold object?' Jill was amazed.

The solicitor coughed. 'I gather that his wife was the more forcible member of the household and Harold rather reluctantly acquiesced.'

Overcoming his astonishment, Robert put forward the burning question that he felt everyone was anxious to know. 'And who were they?'

Henry Arbuthnot consulted his papers again. 'According to the orphanage records, they were split up and adopted by two different families. The names given here are,'—he paused before breaking the news—'here we are ... Brent Packer and Augustus Bart, the latter going by his more familiar nickname of Gus.'

'Brent?' queried Jill. 'That's an unusual name.'

She turned to Robert. 'That's odd. That's the name of your friend who works in that garage, and he said he was adopted.'

'And my friend who used to work for Home Stores is called Gus,' broke in Robert. 'What an extraordinary coincidence. Come to think of it, they look about the same age as well.'

They stared at each other in stunned silence.

10

A TIDY SUM

'We will, of course, be getting in touch with the two beneficiaries,' announced the solicitor after they had got their breath back. 'Although I doubt their inheritance will amount to a great deal after the deceased's gambling debts have been paid off.'

'Oh dear,' sympathised Jill. 'Not much of an inheritance, after all.'

'Nevertheless, I imagine it will come to a tidy sum, enough to provide a healthy income in the years to come.'

'Do you have their addresses where they are living at the moment?' asked Robert, keen to find out whether it could be his friends they were talking about.

'I believe my secretary has already been in touch with the orphanage, so I trust they will provide the necessary information. You seem rather interested,' he enquired kindly. 'Any particular reason, may I ask?'

'If it is my friend Brent you're talking about,' said Robert, trying to hide his excitement, 'you've already met him. He was here when you came to have a look at that new will Jill found. He works at the local garage and his mother's my landlady. I should know her name,' he reflected, 'but she got me to call her Mrs P because it's easier to remember and she's always in a hurry to dash off somewhere or other. And he was brought up in an orphanage,' he added as an afterthought. 'He told me that when we were swapping details about ourselves the other night.'

He put his hand to his head. 'This is crazy – what am I talking about? If that's not enough, my friend, who I've been doing deliveries with, is called Gus. But that might be just a coincidence,' he admitted.

'Well, that's extremely interesting,' observed his solicitor, making a note. 'From what you are saying, it appears that we may have the answer to our little problem already. Perhaps you could get your friends to contact me.'

As soon as he could tear himself away, Robert hurried Jill back to the Lodge, with the idea of leaving her with Rose while he continued his investigation.

But he hadn't allowed for Jill's natural curiosity.

'And where do you think you're going?' She caught hold of his sleeve, anxious not to miss out on anything.

'It's just something I need to check up on. I shan't be long. Why don't you get Rose to make you a nice cup of tea?'

Scenting his barely concealed mood of excitement in his desire to get on and find out the truth, she adopted the pose of a scorned maiden from one of her amateur dramatic roles. 'Wouldst leave me at the tender mercy of a desperado, waiting to pounce on me the moment your back is turned, oh noble knight?'

'Oh, come on then,' he gave in with a grin. 'Only hurry up. I never know where to find her at this time of day – she's probably out on one of her cleaning jobs.'

But they were lucky. They were just in time to catch her as she was wheeling her bicycle out on another errand of mercy, intent on stocking up her dwindling savings, in preparation for that rainy day that was constantly threatening and which she was determined to avoid.

When she finally got the gist of what Robert was delicately leading up to, she uttered a screech of joy, threw her bicycle away and, dusting her hands, invited them in to share the good news.

'This calls for a celebration, my love,' she announced, rummaging in her larder. 'I put this away for the day I won the pools.' She reappeared, brandishing a bottle in triumph. 'This ain't the pools, duckies, but I can't think of a better excuse.' Pouring out a glass each, she raised it in silent tribute. 'If only Charlie were here to see it. Yus, I know what you're going to say. My old man was Charlie Packer all right, or was 'till the Lord took him away in that virus business. Funny, he was dead keen on wanting a son to carry on the family tradition, but as my old mum used to say: he didn't 'ave it in 'im. So, we did the next best thing and chose young Brent from that there orphanage. Queer getting stuck with a name like that, weren't it? But he'd got used to it there, so we didn't like to change it.'

'You do realise, don't you, Mrs P, that it all has to be verified by the solicitor?'

'I know that, ducks, but from what you say, it couldn't be anything else, could it? 'Ere, have another drop of the bubbly.'

'When are you expecting Brent back?' Robert interrupted her flow while she was still sober.

'Last time I saw him, 'e was off looking for another job. Said 'e didn't want to impose on you anymore, what with all that family drama going on. Still, he won't have to now, will he, the way things 'ave turned out? I dare say he'll want to take it easy and decide what 'e wants to do now.' She paused to take another reviving swallow.

'No indeed, what a lucky lad you've got there, Mrs P, if I can call you that,' agreed Jill, filling a gap in the conversation.

'Who's a lucky lad?' Brent himself entered at that moment

and sank a trifle wearily in the nearest seat. 'I could do with some of that. Oh, hi Robert.' Then catching sight of Jill, said, 'Hello, what are you doing here?'

'We've come to tell you something that should put a smile on your face,' she exclaimed gleefully, unable to keep it to herself.

When the news at last began to sink in, he reached out for the bottle and tipped it up gratefully.

'Blimey, I do believe in miracles after all. Who would have believed it – Harold, of all people!'

'Here, steady on, my lad.' His mother rescued what was left. 'Don't you go and pass out on us. What 'ave you been up to?'

'Trudging the streets for miles around, looking for a garage that would take me on. You wouldn't believe the miles I've been, all for nothing – and now you tell me it was all a waste of time.' He looked up appealingly. 'You're not 'aving me on, are you?'

'No,' Robert assured him. 'We've still got to get it verified by the solicitor, and there's still Gus, of course.'

'What, your delivery friend? What's he got to do with it – not the one who got nicked the other day for breaking in?' Brent was mystified.

Robert found himself going over the terms of Harold's will again and explaining about the possibility of a twin brother.

'Blimey, d'you mean to say I've got a twin?' Brent looked bewildered. 'But not that Gus; he doesn't look anything like me.'

Robert got up and signalled Jill. 'That is what we've got to find out. If you'll excuse us, we'd better get on and give you a chance to get used to the idea.'

As soon as they left, Brent heaved himself up. 'I'd better go and have that bath I've been promising myself.' He added thoughtfully, 'I don't know about you, Ma, but the first thing we've got to do tomorrow is to go and see that solicitor and find out what old Harold has left us, if anything. Knowing him, he's probably spent it all gambling.'

'That's him sorted,' declared Jill, linking her arm in his as they set out.

'Hm, I just hope our murderer doesn't find out, otherwise he'll be the next one on the list,' reminded Robert soberly. 'I should have told him to be on his guard.'

'Don't forget your friend Gus, as well.'

'We don't know yet whether he is involved. I'd better ring him – he left me his number somewhere.'

'I think it's time we called a halt for the day,' decided Jill firmly, inserting her key in the lock. 'Let's see what Rose has got hidden away in the larder of hers – I don't know about you, but I'm starving.'

'Okay, you have a word with Rose while I give Gus a buzz. We can follow it up in the morning.'

'Men!' she scolded. 'You never give up. While you're doing that, I'll have a word with Rose and get you a drink to keep you going.'

'Now, you're talking – I'll be in the study.' He started to thank her, but she was already on her way, deciding what they might eat and mentally making out a shopping list for the next day.

Left to himself, he fished out the number Gus had given him from the desk and started dialling. After being put through, he heard the person at the other end shouting, 'Gus – it's for you.' There followed a series of exchanges with someone in the background before the voice resumed, 'And who shall I say is calling?'

Robert gave his name patiently and waited. Then his ear drums were nearly blasted by a familiar voice down the line.

'Robert, where the devil have you been? I've been trying to get hold of you for the past half hour!'

'I'm here now,' said Robert, massaging his ear. 'No need to shout.'

'Sorry.' His friend's voice lowered a fraction, then rushed on, sounding aggrieved. 'Listen, what's going on? I keep on getting a call from some bird who says she's the secretary for some solicitor or other. It's not the Home Stores complaining again, is it? I don't work for them anymore.'

'Ah,' breathed Robert, 'so you *are* the one. Listen, you idiot. I've never asked you this before, but is your surname "Bart" by any chance?'

'Who wants to know?' was the guarded response. 'It's not that supervisor again is it, going on about that delivery to that old bird in the High Street? It wasn't my fault the bag split.'

Robert grinned to himself. 'Relax, Gus. Look, this may come as a bit of a surprise to you but ...'

He went on to break the good news. After a shocked silence, there was a thud at the other end and a voice broke in apologetically. 'I'm afraid the gentleman seems to have fainted, sir. Can I get him to ring you back?'

'No, don't worry. Just tell him to come round to Rose Lodge tomorrow when he's free. Oh, and tell him to make it the front door this time; he'll understand.' Robert sat back, satisfied. One thing less to worry about he decided, so when Jill came to fetch him with a drink in her hand and the smell of food wafting in from the kitchen, he was more than ready to join in.

At last, pushing the plate away with a satisfied sigh, he complimented Rose on her ability to rustle up something at such short notice. 'Well done, Rose, that was just what we needed.'

'That's all very well,' she sniffed, collecting up the plates, 'but what's going to become of us, that's what I'd like to know.

Who's going to pay my salary, now the Master's gone? I can't keep up with it all and that's a fact.'

'Don't worry, Rose,' Jill was quick to reassure her. 'You'll be safe whatever happens. Robert, tell her the latest. You'll never believe this, Rose, but it looks as if you've got two new owners taking over, not just one.'

Rose nearly dropped a dish. 'Get away, you're having me on, sir.'

'No, it's quite true, Rose. Mind you,'—and he went on to explain—'it all depends on what the solicitor says, but if we're right, I don't think you've got a thing to worry about – I can't see them wanting to get rid of this lovely old place, can you, Jill?'

'Not in a million years,' declared Jill stoutly. 'And even if they did, they wouldn't go short of a few buyers who'd be dying to keep you on. Why, if I had anything to do with it, I'd put in a bid myself.'

Robert agreed, yawning. 'No chance ... you're an absolute treasure, Rose. I don't know about you, but I feel ready for a bit of shuteye. Not much point in trying to get some sleep at my digs while Mrs P and Brent are still celebrating. I suppose there's no objection to me cadging a bed here, is there?'

To a chorus of "of course not, the very idea," Robert escorted Jill up to her bedroom, where he bade her a fond good night before seeking out his own quarters. As he drifted off to sleep, he found himself wondering what the inspector would say about it all.

'I see you've heard the latest about the Rose Lodge business,' commented the chief constable cheerfully as he entered Police Headquarters next morning, seeing the pile of hasty screwed up notes on the inspector's desk.

'Yes, sir,' said Inspector Platt, assuming his usual efficient manner, hastily sweeping the offending scraps out of sight. 'I've alerted the local nick to put some men on standby, just in case. As if we haven't got enough on our plates already,' he brooded, 'landing us with two new potential murder victims.'

'Oh, I shouldn't worry too much about it, at this stage,' Mayfield boomed. 'If I know those two, they'll be off celebrating somewhere. At least you've got Harold Williams off your list of the chief suspects.'

But the inspector was not to be comforted. 'I've got a nasty feeling we haven't heard the last of it yet, you mark my words, sir.'

'Steady on, Platt, it's not official yet. I think I'll call on the solicitor to see what he has to say.'

When he arrived at the solicitor's office, he found to his surprise that the news had already got around and he had to call on the help of a local on-duty constable to disperse the crowd of onlookers and several eager reporters.

Showing his card, the chief constable was ushered in to be greeted by his old friend, Henry Arbuthnot. 'Hello, Reggie, I thought it might be your inspector. Didn't expect you to spare the time.'

'We've heard so many rumours, I thought I'd like to find out for myself. Have all the candidates turned up?'

'Yes, I've even got our friend Robert Bruce, who put me onto them. He's brought Miss Gates with him.'

'I thought he might. He's got a sound head on his shoulders, that young man,' declared Mayfield, nodding in approval. 'I wouldn't be surprised if he made a name for himself out of this business. He'll go a long way before this is over.'

'That's what I've always thought myself,' commented the other, struck by the same coincidence. 'You've just come at the right time – I was just about to read out the provisions of the will. Don't be surprised if they all seem a little nervous – it'll come as quite a shock to them, no doubt.'

In fact, the only person in the room who seemed nervous was Gus when he caught sight of the chief constable, expecting trouble following his brushes with the law on several previous occasions. However, this was quickly dispelled as soon as the terms of the will were read out.

'How much?' mouthed Brent incredulously when it sank home. He stared around him, unable to believe his luck. He spied Gus and grabbed hold of him, whirling them both around in ecstasy. 'We're rich, mate, or I should say, brother. Fraternal twins, I never knew that was a thing. I've always felt something was missing, brother.'

Gus surprised them both by pulling Brent into a bear hug. 'Me too,' he said. 'A brother, that's worth more than any money.' He paused, and added with a grin, 'But a house and money come a close second!'

They linked arms and turned to face their audience, all of whom had wiped a surreptitious tear.

'What are you going to do with it?' Brent asked Gus.

'Me? I'm going to celebrate, of course. What about you?'

'I've already done that with Ma – we didn't get to bed until the postman turned up.'

Gus's face fell for a second. 'My lot kicked the bucket two years ago, that's why I'm always broke.'

Struck by a sudden thought, he caught hold of his newfound brother excitedly. 'I know. Why don't we treat ourselves to a holiday? I've never been able to afford one before.'

'I'll have to bring Ma,' insisted Brent.

'So what? The more the merrier,' agreed Gus gleefully. 'When do we start?'

When Robert left them, they were busily making a list of

places to go to, like a couple of school children planning their first outing together.

'They're not wasting much time,' laughed Jill happily. 'Why don't we do our own spot of celebrating and we could pick up a few things for the larder, as well. I don't suppose Rose has had much time to do any shopping.'

'Good idea,' agreed Robert warmly. 'At least that's one thing off my list.'

'Why, have you discovered who our mystery suspect is already?'

'No, but if they're both out of the way on holiday for a few weeks, we can give that priority of mine a rest for a while, thank goodness.'

'I don't see who we've got left, in that case,' began Jill doubtfully. She brightened up. 'I know, you can tell me what's the latest about that mysterious girl you were after. Don't tell me you can't wait to find out and leave me all on my lonesome again.'

'Let me see, what was the name of that restaurant we went to?' asked Robert hurriedly, anxious to change the subject.

'We've just passed it,' giggled Jill, wheeling him around.

Pleasantly lulled by a delicious meal and laden with shopping, the two of them made their way back to be greeted by Rose, delighted at the sight of their purchases.

'All is well, Rose,' whispered Jill as they were putting the groceries away. 'Those two young lads were so full of their good fortune, I don't think getting rid of the Lodge entered their heads for a moment. They were planning the holiday of a lifetime when we left them.'

'Oh, I'm so relieved, thank you,' breathed Rose. 'I know someone who'll be pleased. James was ever so worried about what would happen with the garden when I told him. He can relax now, bless him.'

'Ho, ho, Rose. Do I detect a secret admirer? Go on, you can let me in on it. I promise I won't tell.'

Rose tossed her head. 'Not me, Miss. I'm too old for that sort of thing, I can assure you.'

'Has he never asked you out?'

'No, not him. He's only interested in them roses of his. Talks about nothing else, he does.'

'Ah well, your turn will come, Rose. I'm sure of that.'

'Don't you go putting ideas in my head, Miss. I'm quite content with what I've got. As long as them two young gentlemen don't go spoiling it all. Now they've got all that money, you don't know what they might get up to.'

But it turned out that selling Rose Lodge was the last thing they had in mind. When they finally got back a couple of weeks later, almost unrecognisable and sporting deep suntans, they were bursting with their news.

Brent looked at Gus for confirmation that he could go ahead. 'Do you know what? I've decided to go ahead with something I've always dreamed I wanted to do.'

As Gus nodded eagerly, Brent couldn't contain himself any longer. 'I'm going to set up my own garage business – with Gus here as my partner,' he explained. 'While I look after the engineering side, Gus is going to handle the sales side and publicity. We'll make a fortune, you'll see. It's a cinch.'

'Wait a minute,' interrupted Robert, trying to be realistic. 'What are you going to do about money?'

Brent dismissed the objection airily. 'The answer's staring you in the face.' He waved a hand at the Lodge. 'Look, that's our bank, a solid gold mine.'

'Don't say you're going to sell it?' asked Rose fearfully, overhearing.

'We don't need to; don't worry, Rose.' Expanding his idea, he enthused, 'It's simple. All we need to do is raise a mortgage.'

'Where do you have in mind?' asked Robert interested, despite himself.

'I've got the very place all worked out. It's an old ramshackle place down at Longbridge, only ten miles away. All it needs is a bit of repair work and bringing up to scratch. I could do it sitting on my head.'

'Wouldn't that be uncomfortable?' joked Jill, feeling slightly apprehensive on his behalf.

'Isn't that where Bates's cousin lives?' enquired Robert, trying to visualise it.

'Could be. Anyway, we're both set on it, aren't we, Gus?'

'We sure are,' Gus backed him up staunchly. 'We'll make a great team, you and me, mate. A big sign across the entrance, I can see it now. "The Gus Stop".'

'People will think it's a bus stop,' giggled Jill without thinking.

'That's just off the top of my head,' allowed Gus modestly. 'Don't worry ... we'll think of something.'

'What about, "Heaven Sent",' suggested his brother facetiously. 'You know, rhymes with Brent.'

Thus arguing, they linked arms and, putting the thought aside, wandered off happily discussing the various possibilities between themselves.

'They're quite mad,' decided Jill. 'At least they know what they want, and they've decided to go for it.' She sat down at her desk in the study and opening her laptop, ran her fingers over the keyboard pensively. 'I wish I could say the same.'

'But you've still got all that work of Tom's to finish off. Plenty of time to think about that,' he protested, aghast at the thought of losing her just as he was beginning to feel he was getting somewhere with his other assignment.

'No,' she sighed. 'My work here is almost finished, I'm afraid. I've got Tom's agent coming down from London next week to hand the rest of it over. It's time I started looking for another job – not that I need one all that desperately,' she admitted, 'after coming into the money Tom left me.'

'I tell you what.' Robert thought swiftly. 'Now that the twins are safely out of harm's reach, I can't leave you alone in the house while I carry on with the other task Tom left me. Why don't you come and give me a hand?'

Her face brightened visibly at the suggestion. 'I thought you'd never ask. When do we start?'

'Any day now, hopefully. I've got an agency looking into it at the moment. I'll give him a ring and see how he's getting on. Yes, here we are – Dan Bromley, that's the chap.' He dialled. 'Hello, is Mr Bromley there? Will you tell him it's Robert Bruce. Thank you.' He waited as he was being put through.

'Mr Bromley, if you remember, I called to see you recently. ... You were? Then I've saved you the trouble. Any news about the Hickeys? Oh, don't say that. She's where – in the local hospital? How is she?'

Forestalling a question from Jill, he put a finger to his lips cautioning silence. 'Is she well enough to receive visitors? And how is the little girl, is she managing? You've got someone looking after her, fine. Okay, we'll be right over.' He replaced the receiver and turned to Jill. 'Can you get hold of a taxi? It's at the other end of the village.'

'Yes, but—'

'You wanted to know how you could help. Now's your chance.' He gripped her arm, willing her to agree, hugging his private hopes to himself. 'We've only got half an hour left for visiting. While we're waiting, I'll fill you in.' He was still explaining the background about the family, careful not to give the impression that she might be linked in any way, when the taxi arrived. Grabbing his new miniature tape recorder, he joined Jill and helped her into the cab.

As they were admitted to the ward, he whispered in her ear, 'Apparently, she was knocked down in an accident yesterday, so don't get her too excited; we may only be allowed a short visit, I gather. Leave it to me.'

A nurse led them to a bed in the far corner and drew a screen around them. 'Just ten minutes, Sister says,' she cautioned. 'She's still recovering.'

'Of course.' Jill pressed her arm reassuringly. 'We'll be very careful.'

Robert pulled up a couple of chairs and, placing his recorder on the bedside locker, looked down at the pale face. 'Mrs Hickey – Bridget, can you hear me?'

The elderly looking patient stirred and her eyes flickered open. 'Who's that?'

'It's Robert from "Help the Family". I called to see you the other day.'

Her face puckered in an effort to remember. 'That's right, sir. You spoke to my Sheila – is she all right?'

'Yes, don't worry, Bridget. She's fine,' he soothed, trying to sound convincing. 'Your little granddaughter is being looked after, I promise you.'

'Oh, thank you for telling me – I've been that worried.' She relaxed at the news and sank back thankfully.

'There was just one thing,' he coaxed her. 'Sheila was asking who she was named after, but she said you would never tell her. Who do you think she meant? Was that the lady who used to stay with you, a nurse wasn't it?'

A pained look crossed the patient's face. 'Ma, my mother-in-law that is, told me we shouldn't ever talk about her. She was mixed up with a bad lot, so she said.'

'But you don't want to disappoint that darling child, do you,' begged Jill, seeing the expression of urgency on Robert's face. 'Isn't there some kind of message we can pass on – something to keep her happy and stop her worrying?'

'She was named after my sister-in-law, a lovely kind soul she were. Willing to help anyone at the drop of a hat. Especially that writer feller, what was his name now ...?'

'Tom Conway?' Robert prompted, his heart in his mouth. He felt Jill start next to him.

'Ye-es, that's the one. Swore he loved her, and a fat lot of good that did her. She had his baby before anyone knew what it was all about, and she died soon after. It was too much for her. Ma was left to hush it all up, said it was a shameful thing for the family, very religious she was. He went crazy trying to find out what happened to the wee girl. Had some agency on it, but Ma wouldn't have anything to do with him. Swore us all to silence, she did.'

'Did you ever see that baby, Bridget?' Jill held her hand, smoothing it very gently. 'What was she like?'

'Ah, she was a sweet darling.' The patient's eyes lit up at the memory. 'Ma let me cuddle her if I were a good girl. I used to tell her about Sheila.'

'What happened to her?' Robert couldn't resist asking the fateful question.

'Ma never let on. Said she went to a convent, but she never told us where it be.'

'Wasn't there something about the baby you can remember, something to identify her by?' Robert held his breath, hoping it might trigger a fleeting memory of the past.

The patient shook her head wonderingly. 'Funny you should ask that ... now, what was it? Bless you, sir, for reminding me. She had this queer looking birthmark shaped like a fish, just below her left breast, if you'll pardon the expression. Why, what's the matter, Miss? You look as if you've had a nasty shock. Is it something I've said?'

Jill went pale and shook her head with an effort. 'No, I'm fine, really. It must be the heat or something.' She turned to Robert desperately. 'Is that the nurse I can hear? I really think it's time we went.'

Coming to her rescue, Robert stood up hastily and slipped the recorder into his pocket. 'Thank you for sparing so much of your time when you should be resting. We mustn't tire you out – it's been a great pleasure seeing you again, Bridget. I'll say goodbye for now. Speak to you again soon.'

Helping Jill up, he steered her faltering steps towards the exit where she collapsed against him, sobbing.

'What on earth's the matter, Jill?' He held her close, waiting for her to confirm what he already suspected.

'Didn't you hear what she said?' she asked tearfully.

'Something about a birthmark, was that it?'

'Don't you understand, you idiot? I've got that birthmark, I've always had it. It means ... *Tom Conway was my father*!'

11

OUR NEXT STEP

'You beast,' she said softly, planting a kiss on his cheek. 'You knew all the time. Why didn't you tell me?'

'I wasn't sure,' he admitted frankly. 'That's why I wanted you to come with me. It was just a hunch after you mentioned "Sheila" when we were swapping family histories that did it.'

'How are we going to prove it?'

He patted his pocket. 'I'm hoping this tape will do that for us. Our next step is to have a word with Henry, our solicitor, to show him what we've found.'

He coughed. 'That, of course, means showing your birthmark.'

She blushed. 'I couldn't do that, not even for Henry.'

Robert smiled, understanding. 'Don't worry, his secretary will see to that. Let's see if he's free, after all the meetings we've had with him recently.' He picked up the phone and started dialling. 'I wouldn't mind betting he'll make an exception in this case, when he hears what we've got to tell him.'

His diagnosis was correct, although the solicitor went to great pains at their meeting to point out the legal formalities involved.

'You do realise that however much we accept your testimony, we will need cast iron proof that Miss Gates is, without doubt, the offspring of the late Sheila Hickey and Tom, which will involve DNA tests of all the parties involved? Not only that. If she appreciates it means going against her mother's wishes, she may insist that the recording was made without her consent.'

'Isn't there anything we can do?' cried Jill in anguish. 'I do so want everyone to know that Tom was my father. It would make me so proud.'

Seeing her distress, Robert came up with an idea. 'We will naturally leave the question of legitimacy and all the tests that this might involve to your good self, Henry, but as regards the latter, couldn't we get over it by setting up a fund for her granddaughter Sheila? I'd be quite happy to hand over any reward I get for finding her, if that would help. Would that fill the bill?'

'No, you can't do that,' argued Jill. 'Not after all you've done. Let me, I'll see to it.'

The solicitor held up his hand in protest. 'That's exceedingly generous of both of you, but we must be careful it isn't regarded as bringing pressure to bear in any way.'

'You mean it might be seen as a bribe?' said Robert bluntly.

Henry Arbuthnot adjusted his glasses slightly and rephrased the interpretation more diplomatically. 'Perhaps if I were to put it to the lady in question that a sum of money might be held in trust for the young granddaughter concerned in a way that meets with her approval, it might make the proposal more acceptable. That is, providing that the lady herself is willing to testify on oath that her recorded statement is absolutely correct in every detail.'

Robert sat back, satisfied. 'I'll leave it entirely up to you Henry. We'll go along with whatever you decide. Oh, and before we go, we'd better clear up that little matter of the birthmark.'

Having solved that problem with the discreet assistance of Henry's secretary, Robert left the matter in the solicitor's hands, and decided to celebrate the occasion by treating Jill to a cup of tea and a plate of iced buns at the local café, where they discussed the matter in guarded tones.

'Do you think "she" might agree?' asked Jill, taking a quick glance around to see if there was anyone she knew who might be listening.

Robert pushed the plate of iced buns towards her hurriedly. 'Have a bun, I've tried them.' In doing so, he knocked one of them clumsily off the table. Bending down to retrieve it, he did a quick check of the occupants of the nearby tables. Straightening up, he apologised. 'Sorry, my fault. Yes, in answer to your question. It may take him a day or so to sort out, but knowing Henry, it's in safe hands. I've given him all the details.' Sitting back, he took a bite out of the nearest bun and followed it down with a swig of tea. 'Good stuff, we must come here more often.'

Jill repressed a desire to giggle. 'Are you asking me out on a date, kind sir? This is so sudden.'

Ignoring the banter, Robert cast a quick glance around and spoke urgently. 'Look, Jill, this is no laughing matter. As soon as it gets out, your life will be in danger, you do realise that?'

She looked at him wonderingly. 'Why, because of that ... will?' she mouthed.

He nodded. 'It rather looks that way. Whoever this murderous swine is, he seems hell bent on wiping out whoever he comes across in the family who stands in his way, and it's my job to find out who it is and put a stop to it before it's too late.'

She shivered. 'Does that mean Brent and Gus as well?'

He nodded grimly. 'Yes, they're the next ones on his list, but I'd better have a word with the police now you're involved. Don't worry.' He pressed her hand reassuringly. 'I'll make damn sure you're safe. In the meantime, you're not to mention to anyone about you-know-what, in case it gets about – not even Rose, promise?'

'I promise,' she said. 'After what you've told me, I'd be too scared.'

'Good, I knew I could rely on you.'

At least he cares, she comforted herself as they left to walk back home. She took a sideways peek at him as they walked back to Rose Lodge and felt a sudden irresistible urge to run her hand through his hair, but had to curb the impulse when she caught him glancing at her.

After supper and as soon as Rose had collected their plates and left them alone, he began by setting out strict rules for her to follow, to the point where she felt the prison bars closing in on her. 'Do I *have* to?' she repeated desperately. 'Is all this absolutely necessary?'

'I'm afraid so,' he answered honestly. 'I feel I can't let you out of my sight while this is going on.'

'In that case,' she decided promptly, 'I'll come with you wherever you go – not quite everywhere,' she said primly to see how he would take it, then added teasingly, 'Only joking.'

'Quite,' he answered absently, trying to think whether he had overlooked anything in his determination to ensure she had maximum protection.

'Oh, I think I'll go to bed and read a book,' she decided suddenly, jumping up, defeated by his lack of interest.

Once in bed, she turned over the pages listlessly, idly wondering what he would do if she screamed for help. Finally, she shut the book, deciding that wouldn't be very fair and turned out the light, finding herself dreaming about him well into the night.

After checking all the windows and doors, Robert decided to call it a day and followed suit, leaving his watch handy on the bedside table in case he needed it. As he drifted off, he tried to concentrate on solving the problem of who the murderer might be. But as he tried to make sense of each elusive thought that crossed his weary mind, all he could see was the smiling image of Jill holding out her arms, pleading with him.

'I can't go and propose to her now I've pledged the reward I've been promised to that trust fund of Sheila's,' he groaned. He knew he had to do it when he saw that look on Jill's face and he had no alternative. It didn't make it any easier though, and he was left feeling frustrated at his inability to do anything about it until his financial position had sorted itself out. The thought left him tossing and turning, and it wasn't until the early hours that a possible solution presented itself.

His anxieties were intensified next morning when he was shaving and looking forward to a reviving cup of coffee and a hearty breakfast to chase away his overnight blues.

A frantic ring on the front doorbell followed by a hoarse shout made him miss a stroke, leaving him to stick a blob of cotton wool over the cut as he hurriedly threw on some clothes and rushed downstairs, dabbing at his cheek.

When he threw open the door he was confronted by a worried Bates, pointing behind him frantically. 'It's them village louts again,' he panted. 'I see'd 'em round the back, trying to get in. They be treading all over me borders, ruining them.'

'Are they still there?' snapped Robert, shrugging on a coat. 'Show me.'

He followed the gardener around the back of the Lodge and saw the broken fence and trampled footmarks across the flowerbeds where the intruders had forced their way in.

'How many were there?'

'Can't rightly say, sir.' Bates was affronted. 'Look what they done to my flowers! It's criminal, that's what it is.'

'So where have they gone?' Robert was puzzled.

'They cleared off when they saw me, that's what,' replied Bates indignantly. 'That's the second lot that's tried it on. Can't think what's got into them, I'm sure. I've a good mind to bed down in the shed tonight and catch them at it. That'll larn 'em.'

'No, I understand how you feel about it, Bates, but we'll leave it to the police, that's the best policy, that's what they're there for.'

'If you say so, sir,' accepted the gardener reluctantly. 'But how are we going to stop 'em?'

'We could always put up an electric fence,' debated Robert reflectively. 'That might do the trick.'

'Don't hold with them new-fangled ideas myself.' Robert could see he was not convinced.

'Well, have a think about it. I've got to call on the inspector about something else. I'll have a word with him about it. See what he thinks.'

Bates sounded grateful. 'I'd be ever so much obliged, sir.' He touched his hat respectfully and, collecting his tools, got down to the job of trying to repair the damage to his cherished flowerbeds.

'Hurry up,' called out Jill from the back door, 'breakfast is coming up. What have you been up to?' she wanted to know as she set down a delicious plateful of ham and eggs in front of him. 'And what have you done to your face? Looks as if you've been in the wars.'

'Cut myself shaving. Put me off when I heard Bates thumping at the door,' he admitted.

'Not those lads from the village again? I thought we'd heard the last of that lot.'

'Apparently not,' he managed between mouthfuls. 'I suggested putting up an electric fence, but the idea didn't go down at all well. Bates described it as new-fangled.'

'We've got to do something about it; otherwise we won't have any garden left at this rate.'

'Don't worry. I'll get our friend the inspector onto it. He's always looking for an excuse to give Lark something to do. Besides,' he reminded her, keeping a straight face, 'I need to tell him about your birthmark. That's something he'll want to inspect personally, knowing him.'

'Don't you dare.' She blushed. 'He'll have to take our solicitor's word for it.'

'Only kidding.' He looked at the kitchen clock. 'Time I got my skates on. You coming, did you say?'

'Of course, just let me have a word with Rose, to let her know.'

'And I'll give the chief constable a buzz. I'm pretty sure he'll want to hear the latest.'

As he suspected, Chief Constable Mayfield was immediately interested and promised to meet them at HQ.

Listening to Robert's latest exploits, he turned to Platt triumphantly. 'There you are, what did I tell you? By George, he's done it again.'

'Very commendable, sir,' the inspector commented drily. 'If I might point out, this has landed us with yet another potential victim for our mass killer.'

'Don't be so pessimistic, Platt. Now's your chance to show your mettle.'

'With all due respect, sir, we already have our plate full with existing cases. It'll mean pulling in men from the provinces; we're already fully stretched. You'll be asking me to call on some of our retired people next,' he added satirically.

'Now that's an idea,' boomed Mayfield enthusiastically. 'What about Ted Bird? He'd be just the man for the job.'

'I was only joking, sir,' said Platt hastily. 'I'm sure he wouldn't be interested. He'll be in his dotage by now.'

'Nonsense, he'll be delighted, won't he, my boy?'

'I'm sure he would,' agreed Robert happily, adding to the discomfort on the inspector's face. 'He's always coming up with new ideas.'

'There you are then,' beamed the chief constable. 'I'll leave it to you, Robert, to bring him on board. What say we have a meeting here tomorrow? That'll give us an opportunity of reviewing the whole case.'

'We'll see to that right away, won't we, Jill?' asked Robert, giving her a wink.

'Yes,' she backed him up. 'I'll get Rose to make us up a picnic hamper to keep you lot going.'

When his Uncle Edward heard about the proposal, he doubled up laughing. 'You mean to say old Platt went along with it? It's a wonder he didn't burst a blood vessel.'

'He didn't have any option,' Robert pointed out. 'What are you going to wear for the occasion?' he asked jokingly. 'Have you still got your Det Sergeant's uniform?'

'No,' was the breezy answer. 'I'll wear my old Panama hat. That always got him steamed up whenever I turned up at some function or other wearing it.'

Robert had visions of it turning out to be quite an event.

The proceeding got off to a somewhat rocky start when Uncle Edward turned up wearing his Panama hat, as promised, and not content with that, he greeted his former chief by hailing him heartily, secure in the knowledge that his old superior no longer presented any threat to his future. 'How are you, old cock?'

Ignoring his over familiar greeting and his somewhat

breezy attire of jacket and flannels, the inspector welcomed them all with a strained smile. 'I have been asked to invite you here today to review the apparent unexplained deaths of a number of Tom Conway's family, since his passing.'

'May I ask, Platt, if you have formed any conclusions?' asked the chief constable, anxious to get on.

'Yes, sir. If you remember, it was agreed initially that Conway took his own life due to depression caused by his frustrations in trying to complete his novel to his satisfaction. However, it was established at the inquest that he was in fact left-handed, which did not square up with the entry wound in his head, so it was put down to murder by person or persons unknown.'

'Get on with it, Platt,' muttered his superior.

Taking the hint, the inspector hurried on. 'At the time the deceased met his death, his secretary and the cook had the afternoon off, and the gardener had been called away to look after his cousin, who was suffering from the flu. The last person to see him that evening was Mr Bruce here,' he nodded at Robert, 'who left about 10 pm. Mr Conway's agent called him later, at ten minutes past ten for about twenty minutes, requesting advance information about his latest novel for advertising purposes, and it was established from his autopsy that he died shortly after 10:30 pm.'

He added, with a shade of disappointment, 'Mr Bruce was satisfactorily cleared from our enquiries after it was found he was talking to his landlady at the time, while her son Brent was carrying out repairs to the hot-water system in his bathroom.

'Our chief suspect at the time was his sister, Mrs Brenda Williams, who was unable to provide a satisfactory alibi for the time of the murder, stating that she was staying with friends and after a meal was engaged in a game of cards. However, acting on information received,' he studiously avoided looking in Robert's direction, 'I arranged for Sergeant Lark to shadow a certain gentleman who led him to a notorious gambling den where it was subsequently discovered that Brenda Williams was a well-known visitor. He was able to record a conversation of one of her friends who testified that Mrs Williams issued threats about the deceased because of his unwillingness to purchase a villa in the south of France that she had set her heart on. And what is more, she left the establishment well before the time she had previously claimed, which made her a prime suspect. So, she could have been involved in her brother's murder.'

'How much longer,' despaired his superior quietly to himself.

'Armed with this information, I called on Mrs Williams for further questioning, but she chose that moment to fall downstairs with unfortunate results. At first, we assumed it was deliberate suicide to avoid answering awkward questions, but it was discovered that someone had set up a tripwire to bring about her downfall.

'Naturally, her husband came to our attention as he accompanied his wife when they stayed with friends at the time and also took part in her gambling activities. However, we have witnesses to testify they accompanied him to the front door at the time of her accident.

'Since then, we have discovered that he decided to make provisions for two of his sons, who had been adopted at birth, when he found out that any money he left would revert to Conway's ex-wife. Since his unfortunate death, due to a train accident, this leaves his two remaining children at risk, in addition to Miss Gates, who has now been identified as the missing young lady Mr Conway was anxious to locate and is a beneficiary from his trust fund.'

'So, we still don't know who the murderer is,' broke in Mayfield. 'Can we have a break at this point? I'm sure we could do with a breather. I believe Miss Gates has very kindly brought along some refreshments.'

'What a bore,' whispered Jill. 'Go on, have a sandwich, Robert; you'll need it the way things are going on.'

'It wasn't my idea, going through all this again. I think he likes the sounds of his own voice.'

'He always did,' sighed his uncle, from experience. 'You don't know the half of it.'

'Was he always like this when you were working for him?'

'Don't remind me. I got this every morning as a limbering up exercise. You should have seen him when he really got down to it.'

'Can't someone slip a sleeping pill in his drink?' suggested Jill, suppressing a giggle.

'Steady on,' warned Robert. 'You'll have us all in the nick. Have you learned anything yet, Uncle?'

'I'm still not sure I understand about this will that your friend Jill discovered. What was all that about?'

'You'd have to talk to Henry about that, but basically it said that if anything happened to Harold, Brenda's husband, the money would revert to his former wife's family, because apparently Tom never got around to a divorce.'

'So where does that leave us? I understand that Harold didn't live to tell the tale.'

'Ah, but when he found out about Sylvia inheriting in a more recent will, he got the solicitor to change his beneficiaries, so that any money he left would go to his two adopted sons that nobody knew anything about.'

'What a carry on. Are they the next ones on this murderer's list?'

'Not only them.' Robert lowered his voice. 'But Jill as well.'

'What are you two whispering about?' challenged Jill, overhearing. 'Did I hear my name being mentioned?'

'Yes,' said Robert playfully. 'I was just about to tell Uncle about your birthmark.'

'Don't you dare!'

'What it comes down to, Uncle, is that you're looking at the young lady Tom asked me to track down, and I discovered her relatives live only a stone's throw away in the village.'

'Well, I'll be blowed,' exclaimed Uncle Ted with warmth. 'Is this the young lady we've all been told about – the charming young lady Tom was so anxious to trace, and all the time she was working as his secretary? This calls for a celebration.'

'Did I hear something about a celebration,' enquired the chief constable, listening in. 'It sounds to me as if you caught up with all the latest news, without Platt needing to regale us with any more. Between you and me, his voice is enough to send me off to sleep. Before we break up, as you seem to have been appointed our sleuth of the hour, Robert, is there anything else you need to know about the case before we go any further, that you haven't already discovered?'

'It's funny you should say that,' said Robert treating his question seriously. 'I'm still not sure I get the Sylvia angle on all this. As I understand it, it would appear that someone somewhere is waiting to benefit from all these deaths, and because Tom never got around to a divorce, the obvious beneficiary, as Henry would put it, would logically be someone related to Sylvia or her family.'

'That's quite correct, Robert, so what's bothering you? We've already looked into that, isn't that so, Platt?'

'Sir? You mean Sylvia's lot. No luck there, we've already gone into that thoroughly with the local French authorities. Sylvia's husband went down with pneumonia and died, and Sylvia caught a bug and she's been in hospital for the past couple of years. In fact, Conway has been paying her bills while she's in there. Oh, and there was a son apparently, called

Stephen, who got killed in a skiing accident. We've been through all that, sir. No other relatives. It's a dead end.'

'There you are, Robert. That seems to clear that side of it up.'

'But it doesn't make sense, sir. Who is there left to benefit? There must be a reason, and a motive, of course.'

'Well, if there's anything else you can think of, don't hesitate to let me or Platt know. We'll do our best to find the right answer, won't we Platt?'

'Of course, sir. Anytime.'

'Well, I know it may sound silly,' he paused, 'but is it possible to get hold of a photograph of each one of Sylvia's family?'

'I dare say that could be arranged, eh, Platt?'

The inspector looked bemused. 'A photograph, sir?'

'Yes, I'm sure that can be arranged,' decided the chief constable, already losing interest in the request. 'Look after that, will you, Platt?'

Recovering, the inspector straightened up. 'Of course, I'll see to that right away.' He turned, baffled, to his superior as Robert helped Jill pack the rest of the refreshments away. 'Is that young man feeling all right, sir?' he wanted to know. 'Seems a daft request to me.'

'Don't let it worry you, Platt. I'm sure there's a method in his madness. Now, what was it you were saying about a celebration, Ted? Lead me to it. I could do with a drink after all that. Let me see, when was the last time we had a proper night out – must be a few years ago, what?'

Two days later, when Robert was sitting mulling over a late coffee after breakfast, wondering if he dare call on the solicitor to find out how he was getting on, the phone rang, and Henry came on the line. 'You'll be glad to hear that your friend Bridget was delighted to accept your suggestion of a trust fund for young Sheila, and she has agreed to sign a statement testifying to the accuracy of that conversation you recorded, as a measure of her appreciation.'

'Why, that's terrific!' exclaimed Robert joyfully. 'I can't wait to tell Jill. She'll be thrilled.'

'And you'll no doubt be pleased to learn that it will not cost you a fortune, as you had supposed.' Robert was dying to ask how much when the urbane voice of Henry continued. 'When I put forward your proposal, the lady proved to be very insistent that the sum in question wouldn't be too excessive as she thought it might go to young Sheila's head and spoil her, but in the end I managed to persuade to accept the sum of,'—Robert gulped in anticipation—'ten thousand pounds.'

So, it's all agreed, what a relief, thought Robert. He was still left with a sizeable lump to propose with.

There was a pause at the other end. 'You haven't heard the rest of it. My other client, Miss Gates, has refused to be a party to the settlement unless she is allowed to contribute half that sum.'

'No, I won't have it,' declared Robert firmly.

'Unless you agree,' added his friend Henry, 'I fear the scheme will not go ahead.'

As he wrestled with his conscience, Henry pointed out drily, 'You do realise, Robert, that Jill regards such a sum chicken feed compared with what she is due to receive from Tom's trust fund once the DNA test confirms her identity.'

Robert sat down with a bump. 'What do you mean?'

'Only that she is now, or shortly will be, a very rich young woman.'

'Oh, no.' He groaned at the news, seeing all his hopes of going ahead with his proposal vanish like a puff of smoke.

'Are you there, my boy? Do I detect a note of reservation?'

'No, go ahead,' he agreed in a resigned tone of defeat. 'The trust fund must go ahead. Nothing else matters.'

'Excellent. Then I will set it up as soon as possible. Now that it is agreed, I will transfer the fee put aside by Tom as arranged. Of course, I'm not sure if I mentioned it before, but in that last will that Jill discovered, the money that had been put aside for you has been accruing considerable interest from a stock market investment, so you will be surprised to learn it is now worth almost double its previous value. I imagine that will come in handy if what I hear is true. Robert, are you there?'

But his plea remained unanswered. Robert had dropped the receiver in an overwhelming feeling of disbelief and excitement and couldn't keep it to himself any longer. By the time he had got his breath back, it was almost time for lunch, and he made full speed for the sitting room to break the news.

To his astonishment, Jill seemed curiously indifferent to the phone call at first. 'Oh, good. Does that mean you've come down off that high horse and agreed that it should be shared after all?'

'Well, of course,' he began, 'I only objected before, because—'

'Because of your silly old principles about me inheriting all that money,' she finished hotly, determined to get him to admit it.

'That had something to do with it,' he acknowledged stiffly.

'What changed your mind?'

'Henry tells me that I will get considerably more than I at first expected,' he ended lamely. 'I never thought before that I would ever be in a position to ...'

'To – what?' She jumped up excitedly, all pretence gone.

He swallowed and went down on one knee. 'Propose to you, darling Jill,' he ended humbly.

'I do, I do!' she answered almost before he had finished.

'Does that mean, you will?' he asked, unable to accept in his mind that she had accepted, and it was actually happening.

'Of course I will. I was beginning to think you'd never ask!' She flung herself into his arms and nearly knocked him over in her enthusiasm.

He fell back in a chair, with Jill locked in his arms. 'I can't believe it!' he managed when he finally got his breath back and, clasping her tightly, began to smother her with devoted kisses.

At last breaking free, Jill jumped to her feet and danced around the room ecstatically. 'I want the world to know. Where's Rose? I must tell her.' And before Robert could collect his scattered wits and warn her she was off, spreading the glad tidings.

A few minutes later, a flustered Rose appeared carrying a tray of drinks.

'There you are, Master Robert. Miss Jill has just told me, and me and James are that pleased. You could have knocked me down with a feather when she told me. Here's to a happy future, I'm sure. Oh, is that the time? I must be off; otherwise I'll miss my bus. James has offered to clear up after me, just this once. Oh, and before I forget, this 'ere parcel has just arrived for you, sir. Special delivery. Good-bye and blessings on you both.'

'You got her in a right dither, darling,' he greeted her on her return. 'Here's to us.' He raised his glass to a toast and touched her glass to celebrate.

'Yum, that was delicious. Don't forget your parcel, darling,' she reminded him. 'I'll leave you to it while I have a shower.'

He set his glass down reluctantly. 'Oh, I'd almost forgotten.' He opened up the flap and slid out the contents and found he was talking to himself, and she had left. 'Oh, yes, these are the photos I asked old Platt to get hold of for me. Let's see. This one must be Sylvia, Tom's ex-wife he told me about, and this man must be Richard Willis, the one she ran off with and this one ...'

He held it up for a closer scrutiny and whistled softly. 'I don't believe it.'

Just then Bates, the gardener poked his head around the door. 'Rose asked me to see if you've finished with the drinks yet, sir.'

'Yes thanks, Bates.' Then, after the gardener had picked up the empty glasses and his hand was on the door ready to open it, Robert said casually, 'Oh, Stephen?'

The tray quivered in the gardener's hands as he swivelled round. 'Sir?'

'It is Stephen, isn't it, Bates, or should I say, Willis?'

12

ON TO A WINNER

Robert studied the photograph thoughtfully. 'Yes, not quite the same, I agree.' He held it up for comparison.

'I see you had a moustache in those days. How did you manage to swop places with the man who died in the skiing accident?'

'I dunno what you mean, sir.'

He could see the gardener was getting rattled. 'Tell me, what did you have against Tom Conway? What harm did he ever do you?'

The tray began to shake in the man's hands.

'It wasn't all Tom's fault his wife ran off with his best friend, was it? He treated her fairly, didn't he? Even after they split up, he paid all her hospital bills.' His voice grew hard. 'Hardly a motive for murder, was it?' He reached in the drawer and produced a revolver. 'Lucky I decided to get one of these, wasn't it? I thought it might come in handy.'

His cover blown, Willis played for time. 'What made you suspect?'

'Those accusations against Brent were the first thing that made me think. I must admit, I was taken in to start with, but then I realised it was to distract me from what was really going on. Then those tales of yours about planting potatoes weren't quite true, were they? I've never seen a sign of them, wrong time of the year. And that hogwash of how you look after the roses – just a smoke screen to make everyone think the garden was all you thought about, wasn't it?

'And all that panic about those lads from the village breaking the fence down wasn't true either, was it? Gus has since told me that they came in through the side gate. All done to divert our attention from what you were really up to. Time to call the police, don't you think?'

He picked up the receiver and started dialling, but nothing happened. Slamming it down at the lack of response, he got up and waved his revolver. 'Blast it. Never mind, we'll go to the pub and I'll get help there. Well, don't just stand there, put the tray down and open the door.'

Willis put the tray down and stood back, a curious half smile on his face, as if waiting for something to happen.

Losing his patience, Robert strode to the door and called out, 'Jill, call the police on your mobile phone. Tell them it's urgent.'

'No use you doing that, she won't hear.'

Robert clutched at the door. 'You devil, what have you done to her?'

'She's just having a lie down, after I spiked her drink.'

As Robert felt himself swaying, the other added calmly, 'Just like you will.'

In desperation, Robert raised his revolver and pointed it waveringly. 'I'll get you first, you murderous swine.' But as he pressed the trigger, the gun just gave off a series of clicks and he threw it at his tormenter with a helpless gesture before his legs buckled under him and he passed out.

When he came to his head was throbbing and he had difficulty in focussing his eyes. Then he caught sight of Jill lying unconscious on the back seat of the truck they were in, and his hope died. As he attempted to move, the ropes around him tightened in protest.

Presently, a face loomed over him. 'Hm, perhaps that dose was a bit too strong. We don't want to lose you quite yet.' He loosened the gag around Robert's mouth. 'That's better, can you hear me? Good.' His voice had lost its customary servile attitude and his whole manner seemed to change out of all recognition now that he was in command. 'Let me see.' He cast his mind back to the distant past where it all began. 'You were asking me what started me off in that vendetta against Tom Conway?' He gave a short laugh. 'Not that it will matter now – you won't be able to do anything about it in the time you have left.'

He stroked his upper lip as if by habit, forgetting that he no longer wore a moustache. 'The biggest mistake Ma made was running off when she did,' he reflected. 'She should have stuck it out until Conway made his pile, then divorced him and collected a bundle. Instead of that, she ran off with my old man, who spent most of his time on the booze. That's what finished him off, not the pneumonia, as everyone thought. And where did that leave me, I ask you? No qualifications, no nothing. If it wasn't for that bird getting me a job in the local mortuary, I'd have been on my uppers.'

'Is that where you got the idea of doing a swap?' Robert mumbled through his gag.

'Oh, you're catching on, are you? Full marks, mate. That's exactly what happened. One morning they brought in a stiff they found at the bottom of an avalanche, complete with papers and everything. It couldn't have been easier. His face was a mess, so all I had to do was swap our identities. He had some money on him, so I nicked that and grabbed the next ferry over.'

'But what about that cousin you were supposed to have, the one with the flu?'

The other sniggered. 'Dead easy. He had this letter on him from this bird who claimed he was her long-lost cousin. Turned out she'd never seen him before, so I bowled up there and settled in, as bold as brass. She treated me like her favourite son, didn't want to let me go. Best cover I could have had. Fitted me like a glove.'

'How did you get a job as Tom's gardener?'

'Ah, that was a stroke of luck. I found out he'd been having it off with this nurse, and when he was getting over that and beginning to make his pile, I made sure to run into him at the local pub where he was going on about not having any help. He fell on me with open arms.'

'And that's how you repaid him.' Robert's voice was bitter.

'I was on to a winner, wasn't I? As soon as I got a gander at that will of his, I knew what I had to do. Pity you found out about that left-hand business, I thought I'd covered it up nicely. And if it wasn't for your meddling, they would have put that fall of Brenda's down to suicide. Mind you, they never did manage to pin Harold's accident on me. Crafty old devil, fancy him thinking he could get away with it by leaving his dosh to two of those orphanage kids of his for me to deal with. I didn't know he had it in him. Not that it matters, their turn will come,' he boasted. He added as an afterthought, 'Same as that young lady of yours ... you nearly copped a fortune there.'

Robert struggled furiously in vain. 'You swine!'

'Steady on, young fellow, nothing personal, you understand. Credit where due, you nearly pulled it off – had me quite worried for a while.' After meditating, he added condescendingly, 'It'll feel quite lonely after you've gone. I've quite got used to our little chats.'

Desperate to keep him talking to stave off the inevitable, Robert croaked, 'What's stopping you? You haven't explained why you are doing all this.'

'Why, I would have thought that was obvious.' His eyes gleamed with a fanatical light. 'Once you lot are out of the way, I can claim it all as the only one left in the family. Stands to reason.'

'But your own mother is still alive, surely you wouldn't ...'

'That can be arranged as well,' he said calmly, dismissing the objection as a minor exercise to carry out at some point in the near future.

'Haven't you got *any* feelings left – not even for your own mother?' Robert couldn't believe what he was hearing.

'Why should I? She went and ruined everything by running away with my old man like that. If only she'd had the sense to wait, we'd have been in the gravy by now, and none of this would have been necessary. She had her chance. It's my turn now.'

Robert could think of nothing more to say on the subject. The man was clearly insane and was living in a dream world of his own making.

Eventually, he summoned up the energy to ask the final question that had been puzzling him. 'And how do expect to claim anything when everyone thinks you died in that skiing accident?'

'Simple. I'll put it all down to loss of memory. I don't have to prove anything. They can check my DNA, that's the beauty of modern medicine.'

Robert sank back; the man was an obvious nut case. He had as much chance of proving that as the man in the moon. He asked without much hope, 'And how do you explain our absence? Rose is bound to raise the alarm when she discovers we've gone.'

'I've thought about that,' was the confident reply. 'Your mate

Brent rang up before we left. He's dying to show off that garage he's potty about. So that's where we're going.' He guffawed. 'Come to think of it, "dying" is the right word. Now's my chance to polish the lot of you off in one go.'

A gleam of hope surfaced in Robert's mind as he wracked his brains as to how he could warn his friend in time. 'How do you hope to do that?'

Unable to resist the challenge, the other chortled. 'Because I've got enough explosives in the back of this truck to blow the place sky-high and you lot with it, that's how.'

He slowed as the garage came into view and applied the brakes. 'Here we are. Now, just to make sure you behave, while I set the timer going.' He replaced the gag in Robert's mouth and tightened the cord holding it in place. 'Let's see, ten minutes, that should give us enough time to do the trick.'

He went around to the back of the truck and adjusted the detonator to his satisfaction. Straightening up, he hailed Brent coming round the corner to see who the visitor was. 'Ah, there you are, sir. Master Robert'll be here in a minute or two. He's just dropped off at the local to pick up some drinks to celebrate. Don't wait, he said, go ahead with the tour. I can't wait to see it, sir.'

'No problem, Bates,' beamed Brent, advancing cordially to shake hands. 'Glad you could make it; you're in for a treat. Follow me. Gus is around somewhere.'

Robert struggled against his bonds helplessly.

Just as he was giving up all hope, he caught sight of Gus sliding out from under a nearby car he was working on and calling after them, 'Hi, wait for me!'

In a last frantic attempt to attract attention, Robert slid sideways and butted his head on the steering wheel.

The resulting blast of the horn stopped Gus in his tracks, and he peered into the cab out of curiosity.

'Blimey!' Seeing the trussed up state they were in, he wasted no time asking questions, but got busy slashing at their bonds.

'Quick,' panted Robert as he freed himself. 'It's Bates! He's going to blow the place up any minute. The truck's full of explosives. Warn Brent while I get Jill out of here.' He managed to help Jill out, still dazed and, lifting her up, staggered clear of the garage, making for the nearest hollow in the ground where they could feel safe.

Lying under cover, Robert watched as Gus greeted the others and taking Brent aside, whispered something in his ear.

After a moment of shocked surprise, Brent reacted, snatching up a spanner and lunging at Bates, catching him on the back of his head with it, sending him flying.

All pretence gone, Robert yelled at his friends. 'Over here. Run for it!'

Taking a last farewell look behind at their cherished dream, Brent grabbed Gus's arm and they sprinted for cover before throwing themselves flat on the ground and covering their ears.

Still staggering from the blow and suddenly aware of the danger, Bates clawed his way to the truck in a vain attempt to stop the detonator. As his fingers reached out for the button, there was a blinding flash followed by an almighty roar, and he was hurled back in the explosion like a rag doll.

Surveying the wreckage after the dust and debris had finally settled, Brent heaved a big sigh of relief. 'It's a good thing I didn't sign that lease agreement, after all. That would have cost us a bomb.'

'Leaving aside your choice of words,' Robert pointed out mildly, as he dusted himself down, 'I think we can all agree that justice has finally caught up with Tom's murderer, even if Platt did get it wrong – which reminds me, I think we'd better let him know what's happened.'

'Oh darling,' breathed Jill, 'to think that I begged him to stay on to look after the garden, and all the time he was thinking up those devilish plots to do away with us.' She clung to Robert for support. 'Will you ever forgive me?'

'You weren't to know.' He held her close consolingly. 'That maniac had us all fooled. And to think he was prepared to do away with his own mother!' He shook his head in disbelief. 'The least we can do is to carry on paying her bills, if nothing else. While we're at it, I'll see that she gets a pension as well, after putting up with him all these years. As for that devil, he deserved what he got in the end. If I hadn't thought of those photographs ...' He shuddered at the thought.

'Never mind, darling.' She squeezed his arm. 'You did it – Tom would have been proud of you all.' She turned to the others. 'And don't worry about that silly old lease agreement. How about letting me in on this new business venture of yours and we'll make it a family business? We are cousins after all! Just to start things rolling, I think we can all treat ourselves to a slap-up celebration while you work out the details.'

Dear reader,

We hope you enjoyed reading *Death at the Last Chapter*. Please take a moment to leave a review, even if it's a short one. Your opinion is important to us.

Discover more books by Michael N. Wilton at https://www.nextchapter.pub/authors/michael-n-wilton

Want to know when one of our books is free or discounted? Join the newsletter at http://eepurl.com/bqqB3H

Best regards,
Michael N. Wilton and the Next Chapter Team

ABOUT THE AUTHOR

Following National Service in the RAF, Michael returned to banking, until an opportunity arose to pursue a career in writing. After working as a press officer for several electrical engineering companies, he was asked to set up a central press office as a group press officer for an engineering company. From there, he moved on to become publicity manager for a fixed wing and helicopter charter company, where he was involved in making a film of the company's activities at home and overseas.

He became so interested in filming that he joined up with a partner to make industrial films for several years, before ending his career handling research publicity for a national gas transmission company.

Since retiring, he has fulfilled his dream of becoming a writer and has written two books for children as well as several romantic comedies.

You can read more about Michael on his website:
http://www.michaelwilton.co.uk/
Amazon:
https://www.amazon.co.uk/Michael-N.-Wilton/e/B00EPG3SF4

Printed in Great Britain
by Amazon

72570072R00102